THE VIETNAM WAR

A LOOK AT AN ALTERNATE HISTORY

R. L. Averette

Dedication

This book is dedicated to all the Airmen, Marines, Sailors, and Soldiers, living and dead, both of the Female and Male persuasion of the U.S. Air Force, Army, Marines, and Navy as well as those of the Air National Guard & Reserves, Army National Guard & Reserves, Coast Guard and Marine Reserves, also of all the Special Forces of the various branches listed above, and all civilian personnel who served *"in country"* during the war.

If you can, save for them a place inside your heart, and save at least one glance backward, as you are leaving for the places they cannot go, and try to remember that they, too, loved life as much as you.

Do not be ashamed to say that you loved them, even though you may or may not have always. Take what they have left you, and what they have taught you with their dying, and keep it always as your own.

And in that time, when men decide, and feel safe, to call all wars insane, take one moment, to embrace these gentle heroes, this band of brothers and sisters, who were soldiers once and young, and gave their all, and showed to the world, the level of their last full measure of devotion.

Captain Richard Miles Davis

KIA March 9, 1969

Hanoi, N. Vietnam

Prologue

Actual History (1950-1975)

The Vietnam War is remembered in popular culture as a catastrophic failure by the United States to prevent the creation of a united Vietnamese Peninsula under the Socialist Republic of Vietnam, with their takeover of South Vietnam through military conquest, which is exactly what happened once the Communist victory was complete. Much has been made in historical study, with both fiction and non-fiction film and commentary on the outcome of the war and its contribution to the escalation, or possible lack thereof, of the Cold War. But what if history had played out differently, and the United States and South Vietnam had triumphed against the North? A successful push back against North Vietnam would have involved a complete and total invasion of North Vietnam, and this could have only been possible so long as China and the Soviet Union did not retaliate against the United States in their support of North Vietnam, thus causing the war to escalate into World War III, or so the theory was at the time. If this push back had occurred, how would this have affected the world and the United States' image in Asia if North Vietnam had lost its "revolution" or "civil war" of armed aggression and its unprovoked invasion of South Vietnam? One can only speculate!

Let's look at history as we know it. The Vietnam War wasn't an utterly American war, even though the United States was massively involved in the 1960s and '70s. The conflict itself had been raging even after the end of World War II (1939-1945), once the Viet Minh in Southeast Asia (North Vietnam) had declared its independence shortly after the Japanese surrender in 1946. The conflict in Southeast Asia can only be described in two phases: a half-revolution for Communist independence and a half-civil war to prevent a Democratic South Vietnam, with the initial starting reasons being to wage war against the colonization of Southeast Asia by Japan and France. This fight began with its first phase against Japan in World War II, after the successful Japanese invasion of the region following the fall of France to the Germans in Europe in 1940, thus causing a power vacuum of virtually all of France's colonial possessions around the world, of which French Indochina (also known as Southeast Asia or Vietnam) was a part of. After the defeat of Germany, Japan and Italy (the Axis Powers) along with all of the other nations that were allied to the principle three nations mentioned that made up the Axis Powers, and World War II was over, France began to attempt to move back into Southeast Asia and reclaim its colonial possession, but they found that the people had decided that they did not want to return to the old status quo of colonial rule.

What resulted was a brutal continuation of the war that lasted for almost eight years, with the second phase of the war that was fought against France, and was principally waged by the people of North Vietnam. Led by the new provisional government located in Hanoi in the North that was ruled by Ho Chi Minh and was called the Viet Minh, and was also supported by the Viet Cong, whom were nothing more than a terrorist wing of the Communist lead revolution, who called themselves *"freedom fighters"* but were really nothing more than an army of rogue gorilla fighters.

This war was known as the Indochina War (1946-1954) in France, and as the Anti-French Resistance War in what would become the Democratic Republic of Vietnam (North Vietnam) after their victory over the French following the Fall of Dien Bien Phu in 1954. The third phase of the war that would follow would be fought by the North Vietnamese government in Hanoi, now known as North Vietnam, along with its allies the Viet Cong, (the NLF or National Liberation Front) as well as being supported by both China and the Soviet Union, of which all were Communist nations and or organizations, just as they had been when they fought the Japanese and the French, and against the Republic of Vietnam (South Vietnam) and its allies, the United States as well as a host of other allied nations. This war would be known as simply the Vietnam War (1965-1973) by the Americans, but would also be known as the 2nd Indochina War in some countries, with references to the war with France now being called the 1st Indochina War. In North Vietnam, the war was known as the Resistance War against America or simply the American War. Just like the first war with France, the second war with the Americans and the South

Vietnamese was to be a war fought against opposing ideologies, Communist vs. non-Communist. America began to involve itself more than it already had in its advisory phase with the French from 1950 to 1954, even before the last shots were fired at Dien Bien Phu in 1954. In that fight, the Americans began to supply the besieged French fort with food, medicine and arms, with the supplies being air dropped within the doomed garrison, but it was too little to late, for it did not stop the inevitable. It was clear that the war was lost, and the French surrendered on July 20, 1954. The new war began with mostly border clashes with both North Vietnam, then known as the Viet Minh, and South Vietnam, then known as the State of Vietnam, almost immediately after the French phase of the war had ended. As with the start of their involvement in 1950, the American involvement was strictly advisory at first, from 1954 to 1965, and their role was simply to advise and train the armed forces of the young South Vietnamese government, as they had done with the French. The reasons for the war from the perspective of both North and South Vietnam had been varied, but the core reason was obvious. North and South Vietnam had come into being in 1955 when a peace was hammered out at the Geneva Conference, and the 17th parallel was established that served as the international border of the two nations. Both sides saw it as their right to see to it that the whole of the Vietnamese Peninsular was reunified under their respective governments and flags; so war was inevitable.

In 1964, after assuming the Oval Office as President after the assassination of President John F. Kennedy in 1963 in Dallas, Texas, Lyndon B. Johnson won the election to the office in his own right. Soon after, the Gulf of Tonkin incident occurred, and this would bring about the Tonkin Gulf Resolution.

The Resolution was passed by the United States Congress, which gave Johnson broad powers to conduct an escalation of US forces in the region that would bring them to full combat readiness. In short, just like the situation that had been in South Korea back in 1950, after North Korea had invaded South Korea with intentions of re-unifying the Korean Peninsular under their Communist ideology and flag, but had failed to do so, thanks in part chiefly to the Unites States and to a lesser degree, to the United Nations, so North Vietnam had decided they would attempt the same thing. It was beginning to look like, at least partially, that history was going to repeat itself, but the one factor that became strikingly different was the fact that in Southeast Asia, North

Vietnam had indeed managed to see their ultimate war aim realized, the reunification of the Vietnamese Peninsular under their Communist ideology and flag. The maddening thing about both of these conflicts was the fact that neither one of them had been called wars at all, but had been referred to throughout the duration of the conflicts as *"Police Actions"*, simply because neither one of them had been declared by the U.S. Congress as wars at all. It would not be until years after the fact concerning both conflicts, what they would finally be referred to, and this was what they really were: *"wars"*. By the end, Johnson would not seek a re-election to a second term as President in the 1968 Presidential Election, paving the way for the Republican Richard M. Nixon to win the election. Nixon had tried in vain to turn the fortunes of the war back to the side of the United States and South Vietnam during the Tet Offensive with a stunning series of victories for the US and the Republic of Vietnam following the last ditch effort by the North to gain the upper hand in the war by attacking over 66 cities, towns and hamlets, as well as military installations across the whole of South Vietnam with a coordinated and simultaneous offensive. Although the North had resoundingly lost the Tet Offensive on the varied battlefields that were involved in it, the political fallout of the offensive had turned out to be an even larger victory for the Communist forces than what the Americans and the South Vietnamese had achieved on those battlefields, and all of this had been brought about by the disastrous mismanagement of the war by the Johnson Administration, and the negative reporting of the American news media.

It can be said, that many in the Democratic Party & the American news media who clearly favored a North Vietnamese victory as a conclusion to the war, thus snatched defeat from the jaws of victory, for the United States and South Vietnam had won virtually all of the battles of the war, especially the larger, more significant battles that carried the most impact for the war and the winning of it. So the question has to be asked: how do you win virtually all of the battles, and yet still lose the war? It's simply militarily impossible, unless of course there was never truly a will to win in the first place by the Johnson Administration or the American news media who sought to report the news of the war to the American public with a negative lens, mix these two Factors together and it doesn't take a rocket scientist to see that winning for the American cause was impossible. In other words, the war was already lost, long before Nixon took the oath of office in 1969, but it would be another five bloody years (1968-1973) before ground combat operations for the United States would end, and the war would continue for another two years with American involvement.

Yet the U.S. was still supplying the ever-diminishing South Vietnamese military with needed food, arms, and air support until the Fall of Saigon occurred in 1975, thus ending the existence of the Republic of Vietnam (South Vietnam), and ushering in the newly formed Socialist Republic of Vietnam, a fully reunified Communist nation spanning the whole of the Vietnamese Peninsula. The total American involvement in Southeast Asia lasted from 1950 to 1975, 25 years, with eight of those years being spent in a fruitless war that was doomed from the beginning due to a total lack by the American Government (especially the Democratic Party) to have a will to win the thing, even though the American soldier, airman, marine and sailor did all they could to try and win it no matter what, and we must not forget the American media who did more to loose America's first war by keeping a constant barrage of negative reporting going against the government so that it couldn't have a will to win even if it wanted too, their contribution in this vain, did more for the enemy than possibly 100 fresh divisions of enemy troops with the latest military hardware could have done, all for the sake of their own socialist agenda and to simply sell news stories for the highest dollar.

It is this writers humble opinion, that their traitors one and all, right along with the American people who backed such anti-American beliefs, (mostly jobless, shiftless American college kids) who rioted in America's large cities, college campuses, and the streets of America's smaller towns waving Communist North Vietnamese and Viet Cong flags, enemy flags mind you, while our American boys were fighting and dying for the freedoms they enjoyed, in order to do what they were doing, seemingly oblivious of their own selfish desire to deny the South Vietnamese people their right to that same freedom as well, which was the primary reason the United States was fighting the war in the first place, and with a secondary reason as to preventing the spread of the Communist ideology. Their lack of shame for their traitorous acts knew no bounds as they even waved those enemy flags from the statues of our country's revered Revolutionary War heroes, such as George Washington, as they protested the war and the American government, all the while being favorably reported on by the American news media.

But let's get back to the *"what ifs"* of this sorted history, and examine the possibilities that could have arisen if history had taken a different course. The following chapters will read like a completely different history altogether, as well as reading like a novel too. One history that, at least in this book, actually did happen, at least, we may wish that it had.

Contents

Chapter One

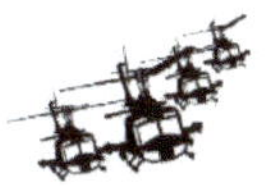

The Presidential Election (1960)

The 1960 Election was held on November 8, 1960. The Republican ticket of Incumbent Vice President Richard Milhous Nixon of California and his running mate, Governor Nelson Aldrich Rockefeller of Maine, narrowly won by 271 Electoral Votes of the Electoral College to the 250 garnered by the Democratic ticket of Senator John Fitzgerald Kennedy of Massachusetts and his running mate, Senator Lyndon Baines Johnson of Texas.

These 1960 campaign posters and buttons for Richard M. Nixon show perhaps the more urgent need America had for a more experienced person occupying the Oval Office than the young John F. Kennedy. This was one of Nixon's strong points during his campaign: his ability to project the need for experience over inexperience. What helped perhaps the most for Nixon was his VP running mate choice, Nelson A. Rockefeller, who proved to be a stronger candidate on domestic affairs issues than Kennedy's choice of Lyndon B. Johnson.

Although the Southern Democrats, Senator Harry Flood Byrd Sr. of Virginia and Senator James Strom Thurmond Sr. of South Carolina, had not announced their intention to run for office, they won 15 Electoral Votes in Alabama and Mississippi and one Faithless Elector Vote from Henry D. Irwin in Okalahoma, which went to Senator Byrd and Republican Senator Barry Morris Goldwater of Arizona.

Harry F. Byrd Sr.

(1887-1966)

James S. Thurmond Sr.

(1902-2003)

Barry M. Goldwater

(1909-1998)

Henry D. Irwin

(1917-1988)

Nixon and Rockefeller narrowly won by a closely contested election; indeed, the election had been the closest since the 1916 election of Incumbent Democratic President Thomas Woodrow Wilson of Virginia and his running mate, former Indiana Governor Thomas Riley Marshall of Indiana. They had defeated Supreme Court Justice Charles Evans Hughes Sr, of New York, and his running mate, former Vice President Charles Warren Fairbanks of Indiana, the Republican challengers.

Thomas W. Wilson

(1856-1924)

Thomas R. Marshall

(1854-1925)

Charles E. Hughes Sr.

(1862-1948)

Charles W. Fairbanks

(1862-1918)

Nixon and Rockefeller had won by a margin of 12% of the vote nationally; he had won the popular vote by only 113,077 votes, for a total of 34,220,984 votes to Kennedy's 34,108,157 votes of the popular vote overall. He had won 26 states to Kennedy's 22, and Harry F. Byrd Jr. and James Strom Thurmond had won two states; it was a razor-thin victory to be sure. It is believed that if Nixon had picked anyone else other than Rockefeller as his running mate, he would have lost the election.

Rockefeller had indeed almost turned down the offer by Nixon to be his running mate after he had failed to defeat him for the Republican

Party Nomination at the 1960 Republican National Convention held in Chicago, Illinois. Nixon, who favored a strong international standing in his campaign as it concerned international relations, needed a strong domestic affairs candidate as his running mate to counter the strong domestic affairs candidate Kennedy had picked in Lyndon B. Johnson, for he had already known that Kennedy had been a strong candidate on international concerns as well, such as the Cold War with the Soviet Union. He had managed to persuade Rockefeller to accept the offer only after he was able to convince him that Rockefeller's agenda on social justice and civil rights within the nation would be far better for the country than the more Socialist leaning agenda held by Kennedy's running mate, Johnson, for Nixon himself had not been a very strong domestic affairs politician during his political career. Rockefeller, one of the few Liberal Republican's in the Republican Party, indeed, he was viewed as the face of the Liberal Republican base, agreed that a Liberal stance on social justice and civil rights as opposed to a more Socialist stance on the subjects was a far better way, in his view, to take on the problems of the nations social justice and civil rights problems. So he ultimately accepted the offer, albeit reluctantly.

Dwight D. "Ike" Eisenhower

(1890-1969)

President Dwight David "Ike" Eisenhower, in the 1960 election campaign for Nixon, chose his successor reluctantly, for he did have some misgivings about his Vice President. Eisenhower endorsed Nixon over Democrat John F. Kennedy, commenting on his choice afterward, he told friends, *"I will do almost anything to avoid turning my chair and country over to Kennedy."* It was originally intended for President Eisenhower to have a more active role in the campaign, as he wanted to respond to attacks Kennedy made concerning his administration.

Mamie G. Eisenhower

(1896-1979)

Thelma C. "Pat" Nixon

(1912-1993)

However, First Lady Mamie Geneva Eisenhower expressed concern to Second Lady Thelma Catherine "Pat" Nixon about the strain campaigning would put on her husband's heart and wanted the President to back out of it without letting him know of her intervention.

Howard M. Snyder, M.D.

(1881-1970)

Vice President Nixon himself also received concern from White House physician Major General Howard McCrum Snyder, M.D., who informed him that he could not approve of a heavy campaign schedule for the President due to his health problems, for he believed that his health had indeed been exacerbated by Kennedy's attacks. Nixon then convinced Eisenhower not to go ahead with the expanded campaign schedule and to limit himself to the original schedule.

Nixon reflected after his two terms in office that if Eisenhower had been able to carry out his expanded campaign schedule he might have had an even more decisive impact on some of the states that he had almost lost, and even some that he had lost as well, but especially in states that he had won with razor-thin margins, thus making for a more impressive win nationally at the end of his first Presidential Election.

Even with his heart condition, President Eisenhower is seen here campaigning for his Vice President Richard M. Nixon at a campaign rally in Birmingham, Alabama, during the final days of the campaign.

Eisenhower did, however, actively campaign for Nixon in the final days of the campaign, although he had almost irreparably harmed the campaign during a statement to the press. When asked by reporters at the end of a televised press conference to list one of Nixon's policy ideas he had adopted, Eisenhower joked, *"If you give me a week, I might think of one. I don't remember."* Kennedy's campaign used the quote in one of its campaign commercials, but it didn't seem to help. Nixon still managed narrowly to win against Kennedy, when he refused to hold televised debates, which had never been done before, over the tried and true medium of radio. He did this to basically punish the Kennedy Campaign for its inappropriate use of Eisenhower's comment, and indeed had used this to his advantage to show the public how the Kennedy Campaign would stoop to such low-handed, typical Democrat tactics, such as the quoting of Eisenhower's words out of context, in order to deceive the public.

Privately, although he knew that he was a fair tactician at political debate, he knew that televised debates would most likely not go well for him, because he had a physical condition that caused him to over perspire even when he wasn't under pressure. If this happened, it would look to the public like he was nervous and indecisive at best, in giving his answers to the moderator, or that he was lying at worst, all the while he knew within himself that this would not be so. In the end, however, Nixon had won the election, and that was all that mattered.

Campaign Brochure for Richard M. Nixon

Richard Nixon for President 1960

Why America needs Richard Nixon?

We need a President who knows the job.

Richard Nixon knows it from experience! In these times of crisis, there's no time for *"on-the-job"* training of a new President. Instant decisions are called for the instant he takes office. Only Richard Nixon already has the knowledge and skill required, based on eight years of direct experience. He has given the Vice Presidency new significance, new importance. He helps guide domestic policy as a member of the Cabinet and is the first Vice President to preside in the President's absence. He helps determine defense programs and foreign policy as a member of the National Security Council, presiding in the President's absence. As chairman of the Cabinet Committee on Price Stability for Economic Growth, he understands how to pay for America's requirements at home and abroad without wrecking the dollar. Richard

Nixon was assigned additional important duties when President Eisenhower had a mild stroke in November 1957. Among other official acts, he took a major part in the decision to start production of our newest missile. He filled the job so well that Eisenhower took the unprecedented step of designating him to serve as Acting President if the President should ever be disabled. He said of Nixon:

"There is no man in the history of America who has had such a careful preparation as has Vice President Nixon for carrying out the duties of the Presidency."

We need a President who knows other nations.

Richard Nixon knows them first-hand! Richard Nixon has traveled the world. Five continents and 54 countries are winning friends for the United States. He knows the needs of other nations, the attitudes of their peoples, and the thinking and personalities of their leaders. Foreign statesmen have learned to respect him. Firm in asserting America's position, yet skilled in negotiating, Dick Nixon, by his judgment and cool-headedness in crisis, has proved himself able to make the right decisions for America.

We need a President able to lead America and the free world.

Richard Nixon is that leader! His understanding of America's responsibilities to the world is shown by what he stands for.

1) He wants to keep our national defenses at such a level that *"no aggressor can feel he can launch an attack without risking retaliation in return."*

2) He wants to continue every effort to arrive at disarmament with inspection.

3) To protect the Free World against Communist domination, he would continue assistance programs wherever effective.

4) He would refuse to recognize Red China as long as it continues its aggressive policies.

5) He believes in ceaselessly working to replace the rule of terror in the world with the rule of law.

We need a President who believes in the individual.

Richard Nixon is that man! Richard Nixon respected the rights of the individual, a principle that has made America great.

1) He believes in creating even greater opportunities for the individual in a free enterprise system.

2) He wants the States to assume greater responsibility for matters entrusted to them by our Constitution.

Because Richard Nixon believes education should be kept close to the people, he favors Federal aid to needy areas for school construction, but he opposes a Federal subsidy of teachers' salaries, which, he feels, would lead to Federal control of education.

He supports housing measures to help private enterprise give America the housing it needs. He opposes the Forand Bill because it imposes direct Federal control over the individual's welfare, depriving him of freedom of choice. He favors Federal participation in a voluntary medical care program for the aged.

3) He is against segregation and discrimination.

As chairman of the President's Committee on Equal Job Opportunity, he has played an important role in eliminating discriminatory hiring by firms under Government contract.

We need a President who can get things done.

Richard Nixon has the know-how! Richard Nixon is a skilled statesman with long experience as a Congressman and a Senator. He knows how to organize the implementation of action, without which, under our democratic system, the noblest goals cannot be achieved. He recognizes politics as *the art of the possible.*

We need a President who stands up for his beliefs.

Richard Nixon's record speaks for itself! Richard Nixon has won every election in which he has run because he was willing to fight for his convictions. There was no question where he stood. As an unknown in politics in 1946, his winning margin was 15,592 votes. His freshman term was marked by his work on foreign aid and the Taft-Hartley Act. The public's reaction? In 1948, he received not only the Republican backing for re-election but a Democratic majority as well. His margin: 141,509 votes. In 1950, Richard Nixon won his Senate seat with a 680,847 margin, again with Democratic support. His 2.2 million votes topped the Republican registration of 1.9 million. In 1952, Richard Nixon became Ike's running mate by popular acclamation. And in 1956, he was re-nominated by unanimous vote. As all his victories demonstrate, Dick Nixon is as popular with Independents as he is with Republicans. He is truly the man of the people - the one man as big as the job.

With your support, Dick Nixon will win again in 1960!

1960 United States Presidential Election

← 1956   **November 8, 1960**   1964 →

Nominee	  **Richard M. Nixon**	  **John F. Kennedy**
Party	Republican	Democratic
Home state	California	Massachusetts
Running mate	Nelson A. Rockefeller	Lyndon B. Johnson
Electoral vote	271	250
States carried	26	22
Popular vote	34,220,984	34,108,157
Percentage	49.72%	49.55%

537 members of the Electoral College

269 electoral votes needed to win

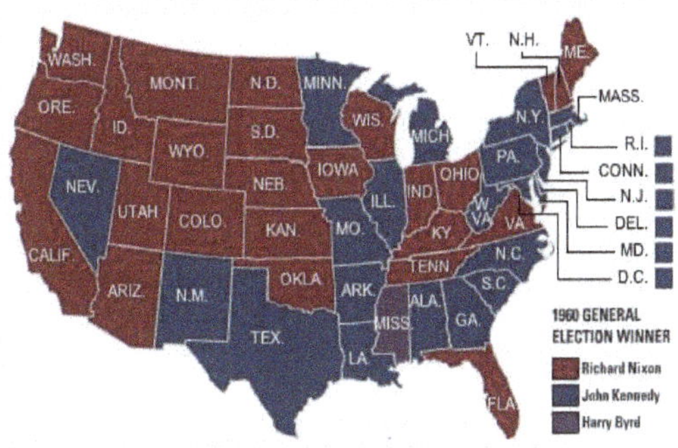

Presidential Election Results

Red denotes states won by Nixon/Rockefeller; blue denotes states won by Kennedy/Johnson.

Note: Light purple denotes Byrd/Thurmond winning Mississippi. Alabama votes for them, too, and they carry the state, but in a last-minute move, the votes go to the Kennedy/Johnson ticket. Byrd/Goldwater gains an Oklahoma faithless elector's vote from Republican Harry D. Irwin.

President Before Election	Elected President
Dwight David Eisenhower Republican	Richard Milhous Nixon Republican

Chief Justice Earl Warren presides over the first inauguration of Richard Milhous Nixon as the 35th President of the United States on Friday, January 20, 1961, at the East Portico of the United States Capitol Building in Washington, D.C. This was the 44th inauguration and marked the first of two terms that the new President would hold before retiring from public service.

Chapter Two

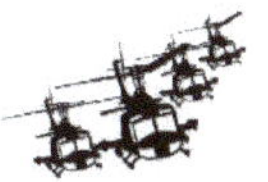

The Situation in Southeast Asia (1950-1961)

Harry Shipp Truman

(1884-1972)

Prior to the 1960 Election and the rise of the Eisenhower and Nixon Administrations, early in 1950, the French asked President Harry S. Truman for help in French Indochina against the Communist Viet Mien, who were being supplied from China and East Germany, for they were fighting the Viet Mien in the First Indochina War.

John W. O'Daniel	Matthew B. Ridgway	Dwight D. Eisenhower
(1894-1975)	(1895-1993)	(1890-1969)

Truman, reluctant to have much to do with French Indochina because he was already involved in the war in Korea, sent Lt. General John Wilson "Iron Mike" O'Daniel to French Indochina to study and assess the French forces there. Chief of Staff General Matthew Bunker "Ole Iron Tits" Ridgway dissuaded the President from intervening by presenting a comprehensive estimate of the massive military deployment that would be necessary, should he decide to assist the French. Eisenhower, who was the Supreme Commander of the North Atlantic Treaty Organization (NATO) at the time, apparently listened to Ridgway's advice after Truman told him what Ridgway had said. He commented on the French Indochina situation concerning the war there and stated somewhat prophetically that *"that war would absorb our troops by divisions."* In the end, Truman did send 50 non-combat personnel as military advisors to Southeast Asia, and some military equipment, but not much in the overall scheme of things. His priority was Korea, not French Indochina, so little else was done until Eisenhower would be elected President in the 1952 election.

In 1953, upon the request of the French for more support from America, Eisenhower, a staunch anti-Communist, did provide France with bombers and non-combat personnel in the form of more military advisors to beef up the numbers from 50 men already there that Truman had sent to 500 men. After a few months, with no success by the French, however, he added more aircraft to drop napalm for clearing purposes. Further requests for assistance from the French were agreed to, but only on conditions Eisenhower knew were impossible to meet, that being allied combat participation in the war and Congressional approval for it.

Christian Marie Ferdinand de la Croix de Castries

(1902-1991)

The French fortress of Dien Bien Phu fell to the Vietnamese Communists in May 1954, following the surrender by French Colonel Christian Marie Ferdinand de la Croix de Castries, the French commander, who would later become a brigadier general.

Even with the fall of Dien Bien Phu in May 1954, Eisenhower still refused to intervene despite urgings from the Chairman of the Joint Chiefs, Vice President Nixon and the head of the Directorate of Operations (DO), less formally known as the Clandestine Service and would be later known as the *National Clandestine Service* (NCS), which is a small wing of the Central Intelligence Agency (CIA).

Eisenhower responded to the French defeat with the formation of the Southeast Asia Treaty Organization (SEATO), which was an alliance with the United Kingdom, France, New Zealand and Australia, nations that were in agreement to the defense of the Southern portion of Southeast Asia against Communism. At that time, the French and Chinese reconvened the Peace Talks in Geneva, Switzerland, and Eisenhower agreed that the US would participate only as an observer at the talks.

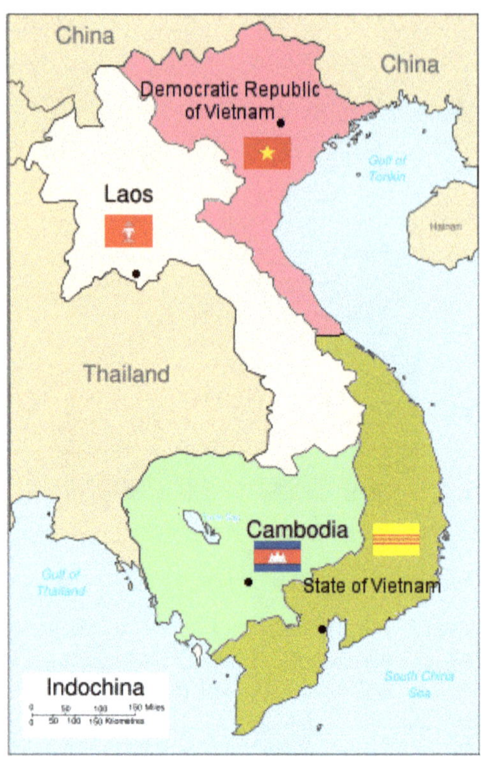

Map of French Indochina after the 1954 partition.

The black line in the middle marks the 17th parallel that serves as the international border between the two countries, with a section within that line serving as a "demilitarized zone." This setup is similar to the demilitarized zone in place at the 38th parallel that serves as the international border of North and South Korea, even to this day.

After France and the Communists agreed to a partition of Southeast Asia (French Indochina) into North and South Vietnam, Eisenhower rejected the agreement as appeasing the Communists and offered military and economic aid to the Southern portion of the region that would become known as South Vietnam. Eisenhower, by not participating in the Geneva agreement, kept the U.S. out of Southeast Asia as it pertained to actual participation in the 1st Indochina War with combat forces. But nevertheless, with the formation of SEATO, he had, in the end, put the U.S. back into the fray, setting the stage for the new conflict that would soon follow.

16

Joseph Lawton Collins

(1896-1987)

Ngo Dinh Diem

(1901-1963)

General Collins' insights and recommendations concerning the State of Vietnam to President Eisenhower played heavily with the decisions the President would make. The help the President would lend to Prime Minister Diem for the safety of the fledging country would shape American foreign policy for years to come.

In late 1954, Gen. Joseph Lawton Collins was made the de facto ambassador to *"Free Vietnam"* (the term used in reference to South Vietnam that came into use in 1955), effectively elevating the country to sovereign status. Collins' instructions were to support the South Vietnamese Prime Minister Ngo Dinh Diem in subverting Communism by helping him to build an army, air force, navy, and marine force capable of waging military campaigns. In February 1955, Eisenhower dispatched more American non-combat soldiers to South Vietnam as military advisors to Diem's military forces, in order to beef up the numbers yet again to a total of 900 men from their previous number of 500.

After Diem announced the formation of the Republic of Vietnam (RVN) in October, Eisenhower immediately recognized the new state and offered even more military and economic aid, as well as technical assistance. Within the next four years that followed (1956 to 1960), Eisenhower increased the number of U.S. military advisors in the country from 900 to 12,000 men. This was due to North Vietnam's support of "uprisings" in the South and concerns that the nation would fall. In May 1957, Diem, then President of the Republic of Vietnam (South Vietnam), made a state visit to the United States for ten days. President Eisenhower pledged his continued support, and a parade was held in Diem's honor in New York City.

John Foster Dulles

(1888-1959)

Although Diem was publicly praised, in private, Secretary of State John Foster Dulles conceded that Diem had been selected only because *"there were no better alternatives."* Meanwhile, the total number of advisors would ultimately rise yet again from 1960 to 1962; the number would swell from 12,000 to 16,000 men.

After the election of November 1960, Eisenhower, pleased with being able to leave the Oval Office and the country in the hands of a fellow Republican, briefed President-Elect Richard M. Nixon. Nixon, being the President's Vice President for eight years, had been acutely aware of the growing crisis that was looming in Southeast Asia. Nevertheless, he listened astutely as the President spoke. Eisenhower pointed out the Communist threat in Southeast Asia as requiring prioritization in the next administration, even above all other concerns. He told Nixon he considered Laos *"the cork in the bottle"* with regard to the regional threat, and that America was not to let its ally South Vietnam fall to the Communist attempt to take over the region, for he believed that if South Vietnam fell, so would go the nations of Laos, Cambodia, and Thailand to the Communist Domino Effect. If this happened, it would probably open the door for the invasions of Myanmar and even India, either from Communist China or even from the Communist Soviet Union, along with a victorious and unified Communist Vietnam helping them. He said that the two Communist protagonist nations of China and the Soviet Union would stop at nothing short of their own national demise, of seeing their Communist vision of a worldwide Communist Revolution realized, and that we, America and the rest of the free world, must do everything in their power to stop the threat before it gets out of hand.

This briefing resonated strongly with Nixon, for like Eisenhower, he too was a staunch anti-Communist. Privately, he resolved to do all that he could to stop the Communist threat, even if it meant war with China and the Soviet Union. He did not want that to happen, of course, for it would mean World War III. This had been feared during the Korean War, and America allowed China, after its intervention into the war on the side of North Korea, first with war material, then with actual ground troops, to at least partially dictate the outcome of the wars end, with a bloody stalemate that even now still holds true under a shaky armistice where neither side had won complete victory.

South Korea had at least survived the conflict and was not conquered, which was the primary war aim of the North Koreans, to unify the Korean Peninsula under their Communist rule, but the war benefited none of the combatants involved. He would do all he could to prevent a World War III outcome, for if that happened, it would likely result in a nuclear confrontation, and no one could win a war like that, but he wouldn't sell out America's allies and or America's integrity and allow Communist expansion in order to maintain a peace with an enemy that, in his view, would never stop trying to tear down the nations of the free world through continuous wars of Communist Revolution until finally they would simply capitulate.

Adolph Hitler
(1889-1945)
Chancellor of Germany

Benito Mussolini
(1883-1945)
Prime Minister of Italy

Hideki Tojo
(1884-1948)
Prime Minister of Japan

This was what Adolph Hitler of Germany, Benito Mussolini of Italy, and Hideki Tojo of Japan, along with the rest of the Axis Powers nations, had hoped to accomplish during their attempt at world conquest back in World War II.

Lt. Commander Richard M. Nixon U.S.N.

(1942-1946)

A war in which he had given his own blood, sweet, and tears to fight and finally win as a member of the U.S. Navy, and he was not about to let all of that be simply wiped away by the Communist powers of the Soviet Union, China and North Vietnam, along with the rest of the Communist countries of the world, including that Communist island country located in Cuba, only 90 miles away off of Florida's Southernmost coast of Key West, in fact, Cuba is closer to Key West than Key West is to Miami. If that wasn't a wake-up call as to how dedicated the Communists were to taking over the world, nothing would be.

Nikita Khrushchev

(1894-1971)

Viktor Mikhaylovich Sukhodrev

(1932-2014)

First Secretary of the Union of Soviet Socialist Republics (USSR), Nikita Khrushchev, made his *"We Will Bury You"* speech at the Polish Embassy in Moscow to an audience of Western Ambassadors in 1956. Viktor Mikhaylovich Sukhodrev served as Khrushchev's interpreter during the aforesaid speech. Beginning his interpreter's career in 1956, he would go on to serve for nearly thirty years at this post, serving not only Khrushchev, but also serving other 1st Secretaries of the USSR, such as Leonid Ilyich Brezhnev and Mikhail Sergeyevich Gorbachev. He also served Alexei Nikolayevich Kosygin, who was Chairman of the Council of Ministers of the Soviet Union.

Leonid I. Brezhnev

(1906-1982)

Mikhail S. Gorbachev

(1931-2022)

Alexei N. Kosygin

(1904-1980)

"We will bury you!" Nixon remembered. This was the phrase that was used by Soviet 1st Secretary Nikita Khrushchev of the Soviet Union while addressing Western Ambassadors at a reception at the Polish embassy in Moscow on November 18, 1956. The phrase had been coined only 12 days after Eisenhower had won his second term in office. The phrase had been originally translated into English by Khrushchev's personal interpreter Viktor Mikhaylovich Sukhodrev, and it was no doubt coined by Khrushchev because of his growing frustration at America's insistence on keeping Eisenhower, a staunch anti-Communist, in office.

Adlai Stevenson II

(1900-1965)

Joseph Raymond McCarthy

(1908-1957)

Former Governor Stevenson had lost to Eisenhower during the 1952 Presidential Election, and after winning the Democratic nomination again in 1956, he went on to lose this election as well. His 2nd loss seemingly angered the 1ˢᵗ Secretary of the USSR, Nikita Khrushchev, prompting him to make his infamous *"We will bury you"* speech, due to his frustration, for Stevenson was a staunch anti-McCarthyism candidate. McCarthyism is the phrase coined in reference to Senator Joseph R. McCarthy, who headed the *"Red Scare"* campaign against Communism and Socialism in the United States.

Anti-McCarthyism Cartoon dubbed the *"Herblock"* due to its creator, Herbert L. Block

Herbert Lawrence Block

(1909-2001)

Khrushchev had apparently hoped that the former Governor of Illinois, Adlai Stevenson II, a Liberal Democrat who opposed the anti-Communist dealings of McCarthyism, which was an anti-Communist drive against known or suspected Socialist and Communist in America, who had lost to Eisenhower in the 1952 Presidential Election when he was still Governor of Illinois at the time, would have a better chance of winning in the 1956 Election, and thus would be more of a pushover to deal with in the Soviet Union's dealings with America, this had clearly angered the man when this hope had been dashed.

No, it was clear to Nixon that these people meant exactly what they intended to do, after hearing such a declaration from the leader of your country's enemy, and with him not even attempting to hide those intentions at all, the course for Nixon had been just as clear for him as it had been for Eisenhower. The Communist takeover of the United States and the rest of the free world was not going to happen, he reasoned.

Nikita S. Khrushchev
(1894-1971)

Mao Zedong
(1893-1976)

Ho Chi Minh
(1890-1969)

Fidel A. Castro Ruz
(1926-2016)

No, he had decided that Nikita Sergeyevich Khrushchev of the Soviet Union, Mao Zedong of China, Ho Chi Minh of North Vietnam, and Fidel Alejandro Castro Ruz of Cuba would not accomplish what they wished to do, certainly not on his watch, and with the help of God, he knew that that was exactly what was going to happen.

Chapter Three

The Military Advisory Years (1950-1962)

The U.S. military advisory effort in Vietnam had a modest beginning in September 1950, when the U.S. Military Assistance Advisory Group (MAAG), Vietnam, was established in Saigon. Its mission was to supervise the issuance and employment of $10 million in military equipment to support the French Legionnaires in their effort to combat Viet Minh forces fighting in North Vietnam. By 1953, the amount of U.S. military aid had jumped to over $350 million and was used to replace the badly worn World War II vintage equipment that France, still suffering economically from the devastation of that war, when it had been conquered by Germany, was still using. In September 1954, right after the Geneva Accords had been sighed in July 1954, dividing the Southeast Asian Peninsular into North and South Vietnam at the 17th parallel, President Eisenhower wrote to the new Prime Minister of the South Vietnamese Bao Dai government, Ngo Dinh Diem, promising United States support to ensure a non-Communist South Vietnam, where Bao Dai was the current Chief of State of the State of Vietnam. Following through on that commitment, and expounding on the commitment that Truman had initially committed to in 1950 to the French, more direct United States aid to South Vietnam began in January 1955 under the Eisenhower Administration, and more American advisors began arriving in February to train the new South Vietnamese military forces, just as the earlier advisors had been doing from 1950 to 1954 for the French.

Joseph Lawton Collins   G. Frederick Reinhardt

(1896-1987)   (1911-1971)

General Collins was the special representative of the United States in the State of <u>Vietnam</u> with an ambassadorial rank from 1954 to 1955, effectively serving as the 2nd de facto Ambassador of the country, following the tenure of Donald Read Heath (no photo available) as the 1st de facto Ambassador. After sovereign status was granted to the newly named Republic of Vietnam in 1955, George Frederick "Fred" Reinhardt became the 1st official Ambassador to South Vietnam.

In Late 1954, <u>General Joseph Lawton "Lightning Joe" Collins</u> was made de facto Ambassador to "Free Vietnam" (the term for <u>South Vietnam</u> that came into use in 1955), effectively elevating the country, the State of Vietnam, to de facto sovereign status, but official sovereign recognition would not come for South Vietnam until 1955. Collins' recommendations to President Eisenhower were to support the South Vietnamese leader <u>Ngo Dinh Diem</u> in subverting Communism by helping Diem build up his armed forces to a point so that the country could wage military campaigns. What he perhaps did not know was that President Eisenhower had already decided to do just that and had even begun to do so even before he had received the Ambassador's recommendations.

In February 1955, Eisenhower dispatched more American soldiers to Vietnam as military advisors to Diem's military forces in the State of Vietnam (now being referred to as South Vietnam). In August 1955, Diem issued a statement formally refusing to participate with the North Vietnamese in consultations to prepare for regional elections as called for by the Geneva Agreement. On October 26, 1955, Eisenhower immediately recognized the new state and offered more military and economic aid, and even technical assistance.

Bao Dai

(1913-1997)

Ngo Dinh Diem

(1901-1963)

Also in 1955, Diem had consolidated his control in the country by suppressing unrest in the Mekong Delta and in Saigon. He launched a campaign against Communists in South Vietnam, in which 25,000 Communist sympathizers were arrested. In October, Diem would advance from Prime Minister of the State of Vietnam to President of the newly formed Republic of Vietnam when he easily defeated Bao Dai, current Chief of State of the State of Vietnam from 1949-1955, and who had been Emperor of <u>Annam</u> (South Vietnam) from 1926-1945, which was then a protectorate in <u>French Indochina</u>, before the French surrender, where he went into exile in Hong Kong from March, 1946 to June, 1948. He was then allowed to return to South Vietnam and assume power as the Chief of State. He was seen, however, as too aligned with the old French system of rule, and he was disliked for his collaboration with the Japanese during their occupation of the region during World War II.

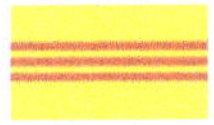

← 1955   **October 23, 1955**   1963 →

Nominee	**Ngo Dinh Diem**	Bao Dai
Party	Can Lao	Independent
Home province	Quang Binh	Thua Thien-Hue
Running mate	**None**	None
Invalid/blank Votes	0	0
Provinces carried	**44**	0
Popular vote	5,784,752	100
Percentage	**98.91%**	1.09%

Note: While the red marker under a candidate of a U.S. Presidential Election designates that candidate as a member of the Republican Party and the blue marker means the candidate is of the Democratic Party, this is not the case in Vietnam. The red marker under a candidate in this country simply means this candidate is the winner of the election, while the blue means that the opposing candidate is the loser. This election was conducted by referendum.

Presidential Election Results

Ngo Dinh Diem wins by a resounding landslide, carrying all 44 provinces of the country. Diem wins 98.91% to Bao Dai's 1.09%. Diem wins the popular vote by 5,784,752 to Dai's 100 votes overall.

President Before Election	**Elected President**
Bao Dai	Ngo Dinh Diem
	Can Lao
Independent	

The defeat by referendum had propelled Diem to President of the new Republic of Vietnam; due largely in part to his refusal to go through with the region al elections for fear that the Communist would rig the election in favor of a Communist victory to have South Vietnam unified with the North. During 1955-1956, North Vietnam concentrated on political struggle, still recovering from the war with the French and influenced by the Soviet Union, then in a period of relative peaceful coexistence with the West under 1st Secretary Nikita Khrushchev. However, by 1957, with the reunification elections called for by the Geneva Accords being overdue, and observing that a potential revolutionary situation had been created by somewhat popular resentment in the South of the Diem government, and fearing that the South Vietnamese government's anti-Communist policies could destroy or weaken party Communist organization in South Vietnam, the Communist leadership determined that the time had come to resort to more violent struggle. In response to this, and in opposition to Diem's anti-Communist leanings, the Vietnamese Communists stepped up their terrorist activities in the South, assassinating several hundred officials of the Diem government. In 1957, Diem's Saigon government also stepped up its crackdown on suspected Communists by arresting another 65,000. The Communists' claims of repression by the Diem government because of these arrests led to the rise of self-defense units in various parts of South Vietnam, units often operating on their own without any Communist party direction, in armed opposition to Diem, as they believed the possible claims of reprisal killings perpetrated by the Diem government, whether actually true or not.

In many cases, this was just another incident of Communist propaganda, designed to continue building on the unrest that plagued South Vietnam, and to the Communist Party in Moscow and in Beijing, it didn't matter if the stories were true or not, so long as they helped to advance their agenda.

By 1962, it would all come to a head as the South China Sea Incident occurred, thus paving the way for open warfare with the Democratic Republic of Vietnam (North Vietnam), and their Chinese and Soviet allies, and other smaller Communist countries. This war would be against the Republic of Vietnam (South Vietnam), the United States, and other allied countries. The War would come to be known throughout the world as the 2nd Indochina War, in North Vietnam as the American War, and in America and South Vietnam as simply the Vietnam War.

Below is a list of the nations that would become involved in the Vietnam War.

Belligerents

Chapter Four

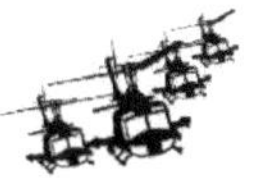

Preparations for War (1955-1962)

Samuel T. Williams

(1897-1984)

Late in 1954, after the Geneva Accords were signed, ending the First Indochina War, about 90,000 Viet Minh troops returned to North Vietnam. This was seen as a step in the right direction by the North and by President Eisenhower as the first step towards peace between the two countries. But by 1959, however, they began filtering back into the South to lead the Communist insurgency, and this greatly angered the President, and it very nearly caused him to go to Congress and ask for a declaration of war against North Vietnam because of this new re-invasion of South Vietnam's sovereign territory. In the initial stages, the Communists organized mass demonstrations along with a few raids on vulnerable South Vietnamese installations, but this was quickly followed by a Communist led uprising in the lower Mekong Delta and Central Highlands that took control of *"liberated zones"*, including an area of nearly fifty villages in Quang Ngai Province. The North Vietnamese Communists organized a shadow government, the National Liberation Front (NLF), staffed by officials not obviously linked to the Communist North, but dedicated to the defeat of Diem's

U.S.-backed Saigon government. The NLF took over in the areas of Communist control, levied taxes, trained troops, built defense works, and provided education, including Communist political education and medical care. During this period, from 1959 to 1962, the U.S. had completed the buildup of the 16,000 military advisors Eisenhower would send to assist the Diem government in establishing an effective military force of army, navy, air force, and marines. They were organized as the Military Assistance and Advisory Group (MAAG), Vietnam. By 1960, MAAGV was training more than fifty ARVN (Army of the Republic of Vietnam) Ranger units. At almost the same time, from 1959 to 1961, the Navy Section of MAAGV worked to develop a viable navy for South Vietnam. Lt. General Samuel Tankersley (Hanging Sam) Williams served almost five years (1955-1960) as chief of MAAG, based in Saigon. By 1962, all was as ready as could be, should the Communists want to try anything provocative that could lead to a possible war.

Chapter Five

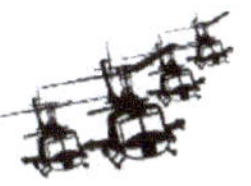

The Bay of Pigs Invasion (April 19, 1961)

Outline Map of Cuba. April, 1961

The Bay of Pigs Invasion was a failed landing operation on the southwestern coast of Cuba in 1961 by Cuban exiles who opposed Fidel Castro's Cuban Revolution. Covertly financed and directed by the U.S. government, the operation took place at the height of the Cold War, and its failure led to major shifts in international relations between Cuba, the United States, and the Soviet Union.

Fulgencio Batista y Zaldívar

(1901-1973)

Carlos Prío Socarrás

(1903-1977)

In 1952, American ally General Fulgencio Batista y Zaldívar led a coup against President Carlos Prio Socarrás and forced Prio into exile in Miami, Florida. Prio's exile inspired the creation of the 26th of July Movement against Batista by Castro. The movement successfully completed the Cuban Revolution in December 1958. Castro nationalized American businesses, including banks, oil refineries, and sugar and coffee plantations, then severed Cuba's formerly close relations with the United States and reached out to its Cold War rival, the Soviet Union. In response, U.S. President Dwight D. Eisenhower allocated $13.1 million to the Central Intelligence Agency (CIA) in March 1960, for use against Castro. With the aid of Cuban counter revolutionaries, the CIA proceeded to organize an invasion operation.

After Castro's victory, Cuban exiles traveled to the U.S. and formed the counter revolutionary military unit known as the Brigade 2506. The brigade fronted the armed wing of the Democratic Revolutionary Front (DRF), and its purpose was to overthrow Castro's increasingly Communist government. The CIA funded the brigade, which also included some U.S. military personnel, and trained the unit in Guatemala. Over 1,400 paramilitaries, divided into five infantry battalions and one paratrooper battalion, assembled and launched from Guatemala and Nicaragua by boat on April 17, 1961.

A Douglas B-26 bomber drops its payload on the airfield at <u>Playa Girón</u> Airfield, prior to the invasion.

Two days earlier, eight CIA-supplied B-26 bombers had attacked Cuban airfields and then returned to the U.S. On the night of April 17th, the main invasion force landed on the beach at Playa Giron in the Bay of Pigs, where it overwhelmed a local revolutionary militia.

José Ramon Fernandez

(1923-2019)

Lt. Fernandez leads the Counter attack of the Cuban

Revolutionary Armed Forces near Playa Girón, April 19, 1961.

Initially, Lieutenant José Ramon Fernandez led the Cuban Army counter offensive, but would soon be replaced by Castro once he arrived in the field.

Che Guevara (Left) and Fidel Castro (Right)

Castro takes command as the counter-attack continues.

Ernesto "Che" Guevara

(1928-1967)

Upon arrival, Castro takes personal control of the counter attack for fear that the invasion forces may be more than Lt. Fernandez would be able to handle. Beside him stands Che Guevara, as he watches Castro directing the movement of his forces.

Pictured is a flight of Douglas A-4 Skyhawks from the USS *Essex* flying sorties over combat areas during the invasion prior to President Nixon's orders to halt all air support for the invasion.

As the invaders lost the strategic initiative, the international community found out about the invasion, and the new U.S. President Richard M. Nixon decided to withhold further air support. The plan devised during Eisenhower's presidency had required the involvement of both air and naval forces. Without air support, the invasion was being conducted with fewer forces than the CIA had deemed necessary. The invaders surrendered on April 20th. Most of the invading counter revolutionary troops were publicly interrogated and put into Cuban prisons. The invading force had been defeated within three days by the Cuban Revolutionary Armed Forces. The invasion was a U.S. foreign policy failure. The invasion's defeat solidified Castro's role as a national hero and widened the political division between the two formerly allied countries. It also pushed Cuba closer to the Soviet Union, and thus strengthened the Soviet Union and Cuban relations between the two countries, which would lead to the Cuban Missile Crisis in 1962. Of all the foreign policy decisions Nixon had made over his political career, he considered his decision to withhold further bombing of the Cuban island during the invasion as his worst, and he had done it simply to placate the opinions of the international community. It was a mistake he determined never to repeat, for it had allowed to remain in place, a Communist government in power that was only 90 miles from American shores, and it had helped to emboldened America's adversaries in Cuba and the Soviet Union to ramp up its next attempt to try and bring down the Unites States in its international game of intrigue and military saber rattling, a confrontation that would have world wide implications, and it would involve Cuba yet again. Unknown to anyone as yet, however, it would also have a more lasting effect on the future conflict that was just over the horizon in Southeast Asia.

Chapter Six

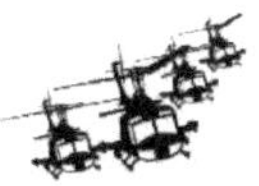

Formation of Military Assistance Command, Vietnam (1961-1962)

By January 1961, President Richard M. Nixon had assumed office, and the steady progress of the enemy insurgency was near crisis levels. The new Nixon Administration continued to increase American aid to the Diem government to prevent a collapse.

Paul D. Harkins

(1904-1984)

General Harkins reorganized the United States Military Assistance Command, Vietnam (MACV), in February 1962.

Military assistance was reorganized as the United States Military Assistance Command, Vietnam (MACV), formed under the command of General Paul Donal Harkins in February 1962. MACV was there to support the Army of the Republic of Vietnam (ARVN) to defend the country. To help bolster the existing presence of the 16,000 non-combat troops that were already in South Vietnam as advisors, MACV included Army Special Forces (Green Beret) instructors and CIA personnel organizing the Montagnards in the mountains. The U.S.-led counterinsurgency effort was based on the strategic hamlet program.

The plan was to consolidate 14,000 villages in South Vietnam into 11,000 secure hamlets, each with its own houses, schools, wells, and watchtowers, to isolate the villages from the guerrillas. As the program got underway, at first, the villagers opposed leaving their home villages to relocate to the sites where the hamlets were being built, but due to frequent attacks on the villages by Communist guerrilla units, they began to see the wisdom of the hamlets and the security they provided. The attacks angered Nixon, and he ordered the Green Beret units to help the locals in any way they deemed necessary. With the Green Berets' help, the clandestine combat operations to effect the smooth consolidation of the 11,000 hamlets, hamlets that were marked for establishment, were still being built, in spite of all that the enemy tried to do to prevent it.

The U.S. Special Forces deployment situation throughout South Vietnam by October 15, 1962, as this map shows, reflects a comprehensive covering of the entire country.

During this same time, the Communists responded in 1961 by reorganizing all armed units in the south into the People's Liberation Armed Force (PLAF), with about 15,000 troops. Many in this force were from South Vietnam, trained in the North and then re-infiltrated, often in political roles as liaisons with the Southern population. By late 1962, the PLAF was large and capable enough to mount battalion-size attacks. At the same time, the NLF expanded to include 300,000 members and an estimated one million sympathizers, while they instituted land reform and other measures in the areas they controlled. As the NLF grew stronger, Diem reacted with more crackdowns in order to try and weed out the influx of Communists in South Vietnam, for this was feared as an even greater threat to his country than the possible military threat that was looming like a dark cloud over South Vietnam.

Chapter Seven

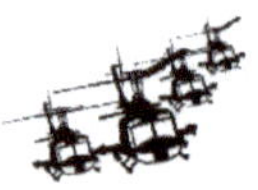

The Cuban Missile Crisis (October 16-28, 1962)

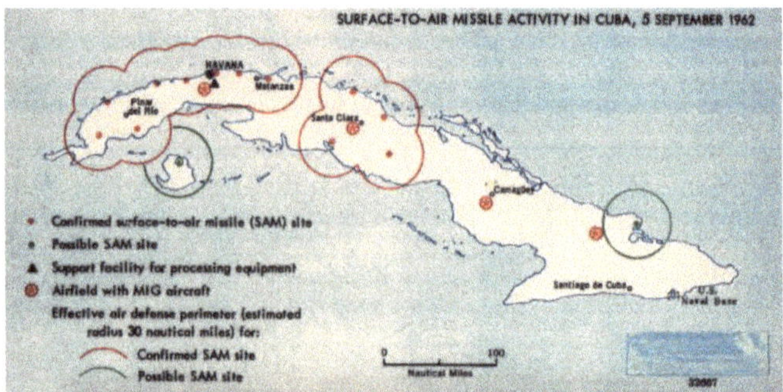

Map created by American intelligence showing Surface-to-Air Missile
activity in Cuba, September 5, 1962

The Cuban Missile Crisis was a 13-day confrontation between
the United States and the Soviet Union initiated by the Soviet ballistic
missile deployment in Cuba. The confrontation is often considered the
closest the Cold War came to escalating into a full-scale nuclear war,
or World War III. In response to the failed Bay of Pigs Invasion of
1961 by the CIA-backed Cuban rebels in opposition to the government
of dictator Fidel Castro, and the presence of American Jupiter ballistic
missiles in Italy and Turkey. Soviet leader Nikita Khrushchev agreed
to Cuba's request to place nuclear missiles on the island to deter any
further future invasions. An agreement was reached during a secret
meeting between Khrushchev and Castro in July 1962, and
construction of a number of missile launch facilities started later that
summer. Meanwhile, the 1962 United States mid-term elections were
underway, and the White House had denied charges for months that it
was ignoring dangerous Soviet missiles 90 miles from Florida.

The missile preparations were confirmed when a U.S. Air Force U-2
spy plane produced clear photographic evidence of medium-range

(SS-4) and intermediate-range (R-14) ballistic missile facilities. When this was reported to President Richard M. Nixon, he then convened a meeting of the nine members of the National Security Council and five other key advisers in a group that became known as the Executive Committee of the National Security Council (EXCOMM). After consultation with them, Nixon ordered a naval blockade on October 22 to prevent further missiles from reaching Cuba. The US announced it would not permit offensive weapons to be delivered to Cuba and demanded that the weapons already in Cuba be dismantled and returned to the Soviet Union. After several days of tense negotiations, an agreement was reached between Nixon and Khrushchev. Publicly, the Soviets would dismantle their offensive weapons in Cuba and return them to the Soviet Union, subject to United Nations verification, in exchange for a US public declaration and agreement to avoid invading Cuba again.

More than 100 US-built missiles having the capability to strike Moscow with nuclear warheads were deployed in Italy and Turkey in 1961.

Secretly, the United States agreed that it would dismantle all US-built Jupiter Medium Range Ballistic Missiles (MRBMs), which had been deployed in Turkey against the Soviet Union. Later, after the crisis was over, there had been some debate on whether or not Italy was included in the agreement as well.

A US Navy P-2H Neptune of VP-18 is pictured flying over a Soviet cargo ship with crated Il-28s on deck during the Cuban Crisis.

When all offensive missiles and Ilyushin Il-28 light bombers had been withdrawn from Cuba, the blockade by the United States was formally ended on November 21, 1962. The negotiations between the United States and the Soviet Union pointed out the necessity of a quick, clear, and direct communication line between the two Superpowers. As a result, the Moscow–Washington hotline was established. A series of agreements later reduced US–Soviet tensions for several years until both parties began to build their nuclear arsenals even further afterward, not long after the end of the Vietnam War.

Chapter Eight

Prelude to War (1962)

Fredrick E. Nolting Jr.

(1911-1962)

On October 25, 1962, the best thing that could have happened for the South Vietnamese government was handed to them on the proverbial silver platter by the North Vietnamese Air Force. Apparently angry that Nixon had managed to force the Soviet Union and its medium and short-range nuclear missiles out of Cuba after the end of the Cuban Missile Crisis, the North Vietnamese military seemingly decides to deal with America in its own way. Flying to Okinawa, Japan, from Saigon, South Vietnam, was the U.S. Ambassador to the Republic of South Vietnam, Ambassador Fredrick E. Nolting Jr. He was en route to meet President Nixon, who was visiting Okinawa, Japan, as he was visiting U.S. Marines stationed at the Marine base there. His visit was to brief the President on the conditions of things within the war-threatened country. While the Ambassadors plane was over the South China Sea, on the very first leg of a trip that would cover some 1749 miles, (1519 nautical miles), with the plane being some 20 miles out to sea, which was some 17 nautical miles, and well past the recognized 12 nautical mile stretch of water claimed by any country as being their territorial waters, thus putting the plane well in international waters, two North Vietnamese Mig-17 fighters swooped out of the sky from the direction of the sun and attacked the plane. There had been no provocation by the unarmed American plane and no fighter escort for the plane because there had been no declaration of war between the United States and North Vietnam as yet, so no escort had been deemed necessary.

Furthermore, there had rarely ever been any North Vietnamese war planes sighted this far south of the 17TH parallel in all of the history of the North Vietnamese Air Force up to that time, and even when one was sighted, it rarely went but a few miles past the border of North and South Vietnam.

The plane was completely destroyed with all except the co-pilot being killed, and he was found near to death as he bobbed in a rubber raft on the swells of the sea when his flight was reported missing after failing to arrive in Okinawa, and having managed to radio a mayday for help and had reported their position before going down, for he was gravely wounded. He lived only shortly after, as he was rescued from the raft and taken to a hospital ship, the USS Repose (AH-16), located off the coast of Okinawa. But he lived at least long enough for the President to visit the man on board the ship, and he was able to tell the President what had happened. The President was incensed; he immediately cut short his planned visit to another military base in West Germany and headed back to the States. Once there, he called for a special emergency meeting of the Congress and pointed out what had happened and the death of the Ambassador. He then pointed out the many other transgressions that had been committed by North Vietnam and its rogue Communist gorilla terrorist units within South Vietnam, any one of them, he said, clearly being a cause for war that had stretched back from 1955, just after France capitulated, right up to the incident with the Ambassador's plane. He stressed that it was long overdue for America to finally show North Vietnam that it meant business about its commitment to save South Vietnam from the oppression of a Communist takeover. He further stressed how stopping this takeover would clearly check the Communist attempt at world domination. He pointed out that should anyone in this august body doubt for a minute the long term plans that the Communist had concerning this dream of world domination, all they had to do was remember what Nikita Khrushchev had said at the meeting at the Polish Embassy in Moscow, Russia back in 1956, and he quoted what the Soviet leader had said: *"About the Capitalist States, it doesn't depend on you whether we (the Soviet Union) exist. If you don't like us, don't accept our invitations, and don't invite us to come to see you. Whether you like it or not, history is on our side. We will bury you!"*

President Nixon delivers his remarks to Congress for consideration on a declaration of war against North Vietnam on October 30, 1962, a speech that came to be known as the *"We will bury you"* speech. This was in response to Ambassador Nolting's plane being shot down by North Vietnamese MiG-17 fighters over the South China Sea in international waters just off the coast of South Vietnam. The incident had been unprovoked and became known as the South China Sea Incident. This incident, and the recent Cuban Missile Crisis that ended only two days prior on the 28th of October, thus caused the resolution to pass, and it became known as the Nolting Resolution.

That quote Nixon had reminded them, had perhaps done the trick, for even though the ruling Democratic Congress could have easily voted down his call for a declaration of war against North Vietnam if they had wanted too, and it was a distinct possibility, the message Nixon had pointed out to them about the Communist threat had hit home to many of them, and although the vote was a slim victory, it was a victory nonetheless, for in the end, the vote on the Nolting Resolution had passed by a margin of just four votes past the number needed for the declaration of war to pass. America was at war, and Nixon knew just how he was going to fight it, he thought, as he headed back to the Oval Office.

That night, October 30-31, 1962, Nixon and his generals burned the midnight oil making plans for the first phase of their response against North Vietnam for the unprovoked attack by two North Vietnamese Air Force fighter jets on an unarmed American civilian aircraft that killed American Ambassador Fredrick E. Nolting Jr. on October 25, 1962, becoming known as the South China Sea Incident. Within hours after this meeting, bombs began to rain down on military installations, fuel manufacturing and warehousing installations, water and power plants, industrial factories, roads and bridges, trains and railroad tracts, and any other targets they could think of, all over the country. Within 24 to 36 hours, the entire coast of North Vietnam was closed completely by American Naval ships as they blockaded the coastline and then mined the enemy's harbors. Even at this early stage, the President was planning for the eventual operations that would be needed to remove the Communist insurgents from South Vietnamese territory, for it was the insurgency that he felt lay the greatest potential for losing the war if the flow of enemy war materials and manpower could not be checked and defeated before they made it into South Vietnam. After all the initial start-up concerns were planned out as the generals made their recommendations, he then took the floor and began to lay out his plans for where these future operations needed to be concentrated. This picture shows the President showing his generals his future planes in the coming months for the operations he knew would need to be made to stop this enemy infiltration, once he said his piece, he then left it up to his military planners to figure out the best way to do it.

Chapter Nine

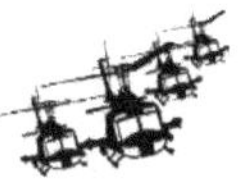

The Vietnam War (1962-1969)

The war began in earnest only the day after the declaration had been passed. On October 31, 1962, upon advice from his generals, Nixon ordered the naval blockade of the entire North Vietnamese coast line, from the demilitarized zone (DMZ) at the two countries border, to the border with China in the North, where a line of American ships and their vast firepower parked themselves just off the coast line and completely bottled up the enemies coast. He then ordered the mining of all of the country's harbors; this was done to dissuade ships from the Soviet Union or any other seaborne Communist countries from attempting to resupply North Vietnam with arms, ammunition, or goods of any kind. He then ordered B-52 bombing raids on Hanoi, the North's capital, from their bases out of Japan. These bombing raids would continue night and day, 24 hours a day, and this was done with the intention of forcing the enemy to the conference table for peace negotiations. He decided that he would not allow the peace talks to be conducted in Geneva, Switzerland, as they had been done during the years of the 1st Indochina War, due to how placating the French had been to the Communists in those negotiations, and he had refused the French offer to hold the meetings in Paris, France. He wanted these talks to be conducted on a fresh basis, and not be overshadowed by the specter of the French defeat drawn up in Geneva, or having the agreements drawn up at the capital of the nation that had lost to North Vietnam in the first place. Upon receiving approval of the Swiss government, he decided he would make demands to the North's Leaders that they be held in Bern, Switzerland, the capital of the country, and still the perfect neutral country to host the belligerent nations of the war. There was not much he could do to stop the Chinese from allowing war materials through their country from the Soviet Union or other Communist countries, or to stop the Chinese themselves from sending war materials to North Vietnam across the border that China shared with the North, but he decided that if he made the bombing so intense over the whole of North Vietnam, especially as close as he dared to the border in question, he felt sure the Chinese, the Soviets, or anybody else for that matter, would not dare to cross the border. He ordered the Air Force to bomb every bridge, railroad, factory, or anything else that could aid the enemy in its war effort, for that matter, to be blown off the map, and to keep it destroyed for good, *"do not allow them even a minute to rebuild"*, he had instructed. Once he had laid out his agenda for the conduct of the war, and what he wanted done, to his military commanders, he then gave them full reign total prosecute the war in the way that they saw fit, for he was a firm believer that the military were the experts when it came to war, for that was their chosen profession, it was not the civilian leadership that should try to lead on the battlefield he believed, during a time of war, it was the military leadership.

He then placed restrictions on civilian journalists being allowed access to the battlefields, for that, he believed, was a recipe for disaster. No, the military he knew, had a corps of excellent journalists that can report on the war, and after the military screening could be done of their reports, to ensure that no sensitive information was passed to the public, then and only then, could the reports be released to the civilian public, and even then, only to a select few trusted newspapers, radio or television outlets that would not be prone to changing the wording of the reports in order to fit their own reporting agenda, namely a Socialist agenda.

Franklin D. Roosevelt

(1882-1945)

No, he was convinced that these war measures were the only way to win this war, both on the battlefield and on the home front. Indeed, it had worked during World War II under President Franklin Delano Roosevelt's watch, and that in of itself was a miracle, for Roosevelt had been the biggest Socialist Democrat to hold the office since Thomas Woodrow Wilson had held it back in World War I, and even then that too was a miracle, for America had managed to win both of those wars under those two men. Of course, neither one of them would have admitted that they were Socialists at all, but the history of their Socialist agendas at home had been quite striking, especially on Roosevelt's watch, and it had been almost as striking on Wilson's watch internationally as well.

Even with the declaration of war received by the North from America, and the major up-tick in the escalation of the full-scale war that America was beginning to unleash on the North after October 1962. The North and its Communist guerrilla allies in the South still tried to carry out their plans to take control of South Vietnam. By March 1963, their initial plans had resulted in some immediate success for the Communists in the South, but the pressure up North by the Americans was beginning to be felt by May 1963, and this was only seven months after the war began with the United States. But the successes of the U.S. were short-lived, at least for a time. Indeed, even though the war was going badly as of now, it was not the war itself that had proved to be the biggest problem the Americans and their allies had; it was the leadership of the country they were trying to help.

Thich Quang Duc

(1897-1963)

John F. Kennedy

(1917-1963)

Thich Quang Duc (upper left) was a Buddhist monk who committed self-immolation as a protest against the Diem government in particular, and the war in general, on June 11, 1963. The photo below shows in graphic detail that death. The photo was made public all over the world, and prompted Senator John F. Kennedy (upper right), former Presidential candidate of the 1960 election against President Nixon, to comment during a news interview he held on his thoughts of the war thus far. When questioned about his thoughts concerning this event, he said... *"No news picture in history has generated so much emotion around the world as that one."*

On the South Vietnamese home front, discord was rampant in much of the country. On May 8, 1963, ARVN troops fired into a crowd of protesters in Saigon, killing nine. Hundreds of Buddhist priests (bonzes) were staging peaceful demonstrations and fasting to protest the war and the Diem government, for Diem was a staunch Catholic who disdained the Buddhist religion.

In June, a bonze set himself on fire in Saigon as a protest, and, by the end of the year, six more bonzes had committed self-immolation. Violence escalated on August 21 when Special Forces under Ngo Dinh Nhu, Diem's brother and Chief Advisor, raided pagodas in major cities, killing many bonzes and arresting thousands of others. Demonstrations at Saigon University on August 24 were crushed with the arrest of an estimated 4,000 students and the closing of universities in Saigon and Hue.

Outrage over the Diem Government in Washington was communicated to South Vietnamese military leaders, indicating U.S. support for a new government, for it was clear to Nixon that Diem and his brother had gone too far in their personal vendetta against all things Buddhist.

The President feared that if Diem remained in power, he would threaten to derail all the positive gains that had occurred thus far in the war for America and South Vietnam, for there had been other incidents in the past, before and after the beginning of the war, where Diem had caused strife among his own people with his provocative actions. Diem had always been a staunch anti-Communist, and that played well in America's interest so far, and had Diem stuck to his policies of dealing with the Communists within his country without these anti-Buddhist actions of his, all would have been well, but when he insisted on his outright persecution of all who were not Catholic, he became a liability.

Henry Cabot Lodge

(1902-1985)

Lodge becomes the new U.S. Ambassador to the Republic of Vietnam following the death of Ambassador Nolting during the South China Sea Incident. Along with the Nixon Administration and the CIA, Lodge is instrumental in encouraging a coup that would remove President Diem from office and replace him with the more agreeable General Duong Van Minh as the new South Vietnamese President.

The Nixon Administration, through the CIA and the new American Ambassador of South Vietnam, Henry Cabot Lodge, who had assumed the post after the death of Ambassador Fredrick E. Nolting Jr. who's plane had been shot down by enemy fighters in 1962, the very act that helped to propel America to finally declare war on North Vietnam, and known as the South China Sea Incident, had encouraged a coup d'etat in early October 1963, in which Diem and Nhu were assassinated in November. General Duong Van Minh took over the government, and the U.S. was obligated to support him, even though they did protest the assignation as the means for removing Diem, for they had preferred

51

arrest and exile from the country. Nevertheless, Minh had proved a better man for America to deal with for the duration of the war.

Duong Van Minh

(1916-2001)

Ngo Dinh Nhu

(1910-1963)

After the coup d'etat, which began on October 1, 1963, General Minh took over the government, and soon he was placed as the 2nd President of the Republic of Vietnam. Through his leadership, he brought about the successful conclusion of the war in April 1969 with the total capitulation and surrender of North Vietnam. Ngo Dinh Nhu was the brother of President Ngo Dinh Diem; he too was assassinated along with his brother on November 2, 1963.

This grim photo shows the complete violence of Diem's assassination during the coup d'etat. Ngo Dinh Diem died on November 2, 1963.

1963 Republic of Vietnam coup d'etat

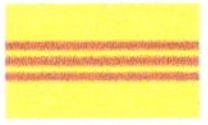

← 1963 **October 01, 1963** 1969 →

Nominee	**Duong Van Minh**	Ngo Dinh Diem
Party	Military	Can Lao
Home province	My Tho	Quang Bình
Running mate	**None**	None
Invalid/ blank Votes	0	0
Provinces carried	0	0
Popular vote	0	0
Percentage	0	0

Note: While the red marker under a candidate of a U.S. Presidential Election designates that candidate as a member of the Republican Party and the blue designation means the candidate is of the

Democratic Party, this is not the case in Vietnam. The red designation under a candidate in this country simply means this candidate is the winner of the election, while the blue designation means that the opposing candidate is the loser. This election was the result of a military coup d'etat.

Presidential coup d'etat Results

After it was learned that suspected election fraud had been committed during the referendum election of 1955, and after committing rampant corruption within the government, as well as religious oppression against all religions except Catholicism. The South Vietnamese military, backed by the United States because they now viewed Diem as a liability who could lose the war for the South, conducted a military coup d'etat against Diem and his brother <u>Ngo Dinh Nhu</u>. The coup began on October 1, 1963, and ended on November 2, 1963, after Diem and his brother Ngo Dinh Nhu were assassinated. Minh becomes President soon after and leads the country to a victorious conclusion in 1969.

President Before coup d'etat	**President After coup d'etat**
Ngo Dinh Diem <u>Can Lao</u>	Duong Van Minh Military

By March 1964, the Communists had managed to rebound and controlled over forty percent of the country in South Vietnam, due to the unrest of the corrupt Diem government. So-called "liberated zones" from the Central Highlands to the edge of the Mekong Delta, containing half the population, were now in control of the Communists. The PLAF forces, now called the *"Viet Cong," short for "Viet Nam Cong San," meaning "Vietnamese Communist,"* had grown to 35,000 guerrillas and 80,000 irregulars. They were supplied and augmented by the completion of a route through Laos and Cambodia known as the Ho Chi Minh Trail, a trail that had been built from 1959 and remained open until 1969, when the U.S. and South Vietnam finally managed to close the trail. Despite an ARVN force of 300,000 soldiers, U.S. aircraft over South Vietnam were fired upon by Chinese and Soviet made anti-aircraft artillery, and terrorist bombs were even exploding in Saigon, and the area controlled by the Viet Cong continued to increase.

During all of the non-committal attitude of the Dai government, and the corruption and dictatorial oppression of the Diem government, the government in Saigon ended up changing at least three times, with Bao Dai, Ngo Dinh Diem, and Duong Van Minh. Fortunately for the fledging republic, their government finally got it right once Minh's administration came to power.

The Presidential Election (1964)

On the American home front, 1964 was an election year, and although Nixon was enjoying a decided up-tick to his popularity concerning the measured successes the U.S. was having in the war, at least until March of the year, when the fortunes of the war seemed to be smiling on the Communist once again, Nixon was beginning to worry about the upcoming election in November. The democrats used this unfortunate turn of events to hammer home the need to end the war, or at least that it was time for new leadership that could win the war the way they saw that it could be won. They tried to turn the public against the present administration in particular, and the war in general, and this was their undoing. The American public was having none of it. There had been small, Socialist led movements of radical American college students, backed by their Socialist teachers and some Socialist American news media people who were angry that Nixon had kept them off the battlefields so that they could have unfettered access to reporting the way they saw fit, that is according to their Socialist way of thinking, but it had never grown to any size to make a difference, but it could, if the war went badly, Nixon realized. He shuddered to think of the untold damage civilian journalists and the mainstream news media could do to the war effort and to public morale for the war if they were allowed to make unfettered reports, such as the report that leaked out about the Buddhist monks killing themselves as a protest against the war. Never mind that their chief reason for doing such a thing had been the opposition they had against the Diem government. Fortunately, he had managed to stem that problem before it had had a chance to grow into something that could not be contained. The fact remained, however, that the American public was still solidly behind the President and the war; this rendered Nixon's worries about re-election unnecessary.

Even the Liberal and Socialist leaning Time magazine, certainly no friend to Nixon or the Republican GOP, predicted that Nixon would win a landslide in his 1964 re-election bid, for they knew that he was extremely popular despite the setbacks earlier in the war, for they knew that the U.S. Military and the President was winning the Vietnam War. Little did they realize just how big that landslide was going to be?

Nominee	**Richard M. Nixon**	George C. Wallace
Party	Republican	Democratic
Home state	California	Alabama
Running mate	**Nelson A. Rockefeller**	James S. Thurmond Sr.
Electoral vote	**486**	52
States carried	**44 + DC**	6
Popular vote	**63,055,622**	9,901,118
Percentage	**68.1%**	13.5%

538 members of the <u>Electoral College</u>

270 electoral votes needed to win

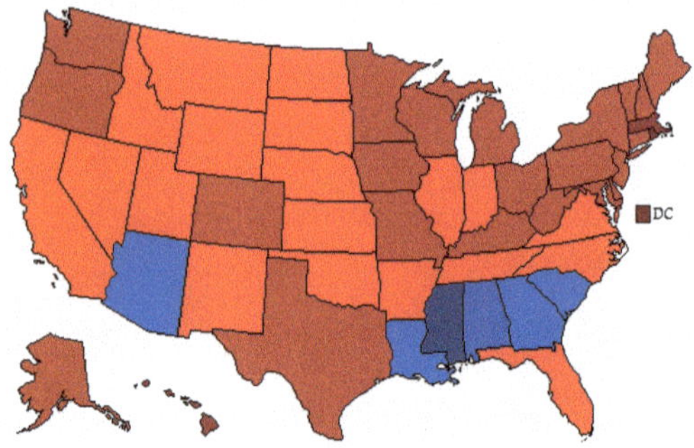

Presidential Election Results

Red denotes states won by Nixon/Rockefeller, and Blue denotes those won by Wallace/Thurmond.

Note: Dark Red denotes solid support for the Nixon/Rockefeller ticket, light red denotes lighter support for the ticket, but the states involved were still carried by Nixon and Rockefeller. Dark blue denotes solid support for the Wallace/Thurmond ticket, and light blue denotes lighter support for the ticket, but the states involved were still carried by Wallace and Thurmond.

Note: In a strange quirk of political fate, the District of Columbia (DC), typically a solid Democratic stronghold, voted Republican to everyone's surprise, including Nixon himself, thus causing the district to go solidly for Nixon in this election cycle.

<table>
<tr><td>President Before Election</td><td>Elected President</td></tr>
<tr><td>Richard Milhous Nixon
Republican</td><td>Richard Milhous Nixon
Republican</td></tr>
</table>

James Strom Thurmond

(1902-2003)

Fielding Lewis Wright

(1895-1956)

James Strom Thurmond Sr., once a Democrat prior to the 1948 Presidential Election, opted to run on a third-party ticket after he became convinced that the Democratic Party did not hold true to the wishes of Southern Democrats.

Hence, the formation of the States Rights "Democratic" Party, he was picked to run for President on this party ticket, which was also known as the Dixiecrats Party, and he chose Gov. Fielding Lewis Wright of Mississippi as his running mate. Unfortunately, the Thurmond/Wright campaign did not prevail on Election Day; the Thurmond/Wright ticket carried the previously solid Democratic states of Louisiana, Mississippi, Alabama, and Thurmond's own home state of South Carolina, plus one faithless elector vote from Tennessee, four states in total. The ticket received 1,176,023 popular votes and 39 electoral votes, for an overall national percentage of 2.4%. Nevertheless, he remains with the States' Rights Party for the next 16 years, from 1948 until 1964. Although the States' Rights party had always viewed itself as a Southern version of the Democratic Party, Thurmond reluctantly accepts Wallace's offer to run with him on the Democratic Party ticket in the 1964 election, and thus rejoins the Democratic Party. After the loss of the 1964 election, Thurmond switched parties for the last time. He joined the Republican Party and remained with this party for the duration of his political life, from 1964 till his death in 2003 at the age of 100.

Chief Justice of the Supreme Court Earl Warren administers the oath of office of the second inauguration of **Richard Milhous Nixon** as the 35th President of the United States. It was held on Wednesday, January 20, 1965, again at the East Portico of the United States Capitol in Washington, D.C. This was the 45th inauguration and marked the second of two terms that he would hold in office after he would go on to win the largest landslide victory in U.S. history on Tuesday, November 3, 1964 as he defeated Gov. George Wallace of Alabama and his running mate Gov. James Strom Thurmond of South Carolina. Upon the completion of his second term, he returns to California and retires from public service.

After Nixon took the oath of office in January 1965, the fortunes of war took an about-face and changed again for the U.S. and South Vietnam, and this time they never lost the winning momentum again. After having successfully negotiated with the Americans during the 1962 Cuban Missile Crisis and having received most of what they had wanted in the agreements, the Soviet Union, not wanting to sour the good relations the U.S. and Russia had achieved during those meetings, decided that it was time to forget about North Vietnam and go on to other pursuits. China, on the other hand, had taken a little stronger stance and had not wanted to give in, but the Soviet Union convinced China that it was in their best interest to let this one go, for after loosing in Cuba, and loosing its missile advantage in Turkey, they knew the Americans were in no mood to tolerate their medaling in Southeast Asia. Seeing the direction of the prevailing winds that were blowing, China finally began, as had Russia, to see that the war was all but lost for North Vietnam.

Within months after Russia and China's decisions, all of the other Communist nations supporting North Vietnam ceased their support as well; once they were warned by the two larger Communist nations that trade embargos would become effective against them if they didn't. In April 1965, they warn their North Vietnamese friends that they need to seek a negotiated peace with America and South Vietnam, and finally recognize South Vietnam's sovereign right to self rule, for they believe that if the war prevails, America will surly invade the North, and there will be nothing to stop them, for they will not commit combat ground troops to help them in a fruitless war that serves no purpose at this point, and that they stand to loose even their existence as a nation in the North, for South Vietnam still hopes to unite the Vietnamese Peninsular under their rule as well. They withdraw their support of the Northern regime, but the North Vietnamese leaders refuse to let go of their dreams of acquiring the whole of the Vietnamese Peninsular, and the war continues. The Communists in the South, however, still had a few tricks up their sleeves. Even with the disastrous outcome that had happened in April with the Soviet Union and China, they managed to sow even more discord in the South.

Since the removal of China and the Soviet Union, along with all the other Communist allied nations that had left North Vietnam to its fate in January 1965, the Ho Chi Minh Trail was quickly becoming the key to victory in the war itself. The trail had been built by the North to be a logistical *"highway"* to funnel arms, ammunition, food, and all other manner of war material from the North through Laos and Cambodia to South Vietnam to supply the troops it had there as well as the insurgent forces that fought for the North. But the war material was already beginning to dry up, as the goods they had stored prior to the departure of their allies from the conflict continued a steady flow down the trail, and it was a flow that could not long endure. Couple this with the constant bombardment of the trail by U.S. and South Vietnamese war planes on a regular basis all along the trail from the South Vietnamese border of Cambodia to the Laotian border with North Vietnam, and it did not take a genius to figure out that it was only a matter of time before North Vietnam would have to consider suing for peace.

Ho Chi Minh Trail (1959-1969)

Map of the Ho Chi Minh Trail (1965)

The Ho Chi Minh Trail, a trail that had been built from 1959 and remained open until 1969, served as the primary route for war material and troops flowing down from North Vietnam to support the insurgency in the South. The U.S. and South Vietnam finally managed to close the trail shortly before the end of the War.

If 1965 can be considered the turning point in the war for the United States and South Vietnam, then 1968 was the beginning of the end for North Vietnam, and the key that unlocked the door to North Vietnam was the Ho Chi Minh Trail. The trail had been considered by the Communists as the key that would win the war for them in North Vietnam, and it most likely would have been if the North's allies had not decided to jump ship. But the trail was now working against them, for it was bleeding them dry of quickly diminishing supplies, supplies they no longer received after their allies had left them. The war continued to progress well for the U.S., South Vietnam, and its allies throughout the remainder of 1965 and on through 1966 and 1967. The U.S., with its superior air power based at multiple air bases in South Vietnam, as well as Thailand and Japan, had almost completely destroyed the enemy's ability to make war against them with their ground-to-air missile bases, and their air force had virtually ceased to exist. With the North Vietnamese Navy all but nonexistent as well, the U.S. Navy, with its aircraft carriers, had parked itself a little away from the cruisers and destroyers that manned the blockade of the enemy's coastline, and continued to pound the enemy from the sea. And with all of this, North Vietnam still refused to accept the fact that the war was lost for them, and that further conflict was pointless. The meeting at the Bern, Switzerland Peace Conference, which had been going on only days after the war began in 1962, netted few results as the North continued their resistance to give up the fight. It seemed that they would rather face the risk of complete destruction than to give up their dream of a unified Communist Vietnamese Peninsular under their flag and rule.

The Underground Tunnels of Cu Chi (1967-1969)

During the war in French Indochina, thousands of people in the Vietnamese province of Cu Chi lived in an elaborate network of underground tunnels. The tunnels were used by Viet Cong guerrillas as hiding spots during combat, as well as serving as communication and supply routes, hospitals, food and weapon caches, and living quarters for numerous guerrilla fighters. The tunnel systems were of great importance to the Viet Cong in their resistance to first the French and then the American forces in both the 1st and 2nd Indochina Wars, but even though the tunnel systems played a major role in North Vietnam's ongoing wars with France and America, and although it played a major part in North Vietnam winning it's war against the French, it would prove unable to repeat it's tactical advantage for a win against the American's. The Cu Chi tunnels were built over a period of 24 years that began sometime in the late 1940s during the onset of the war against the French. The excavations were used mostly for communication between villages and to evade French army sweeps of the area. When the National Liberation Front (NLF) insurgency began around 1960, two years before the start of the 2nd Indochina War (the Vietnam War) began in 1962, the leaders of the North began preparations for a possible new war with America.

The old tunnels were repaired, and new extensions were excavated. Within the two years before the new war started, the tunnel system assumed enormous strategic importance for the insurgency war that was about to get underway, just as it had been against the French in the previous war, and most of the Cu Chi district and the nearby area came under firm Viet Cong control.

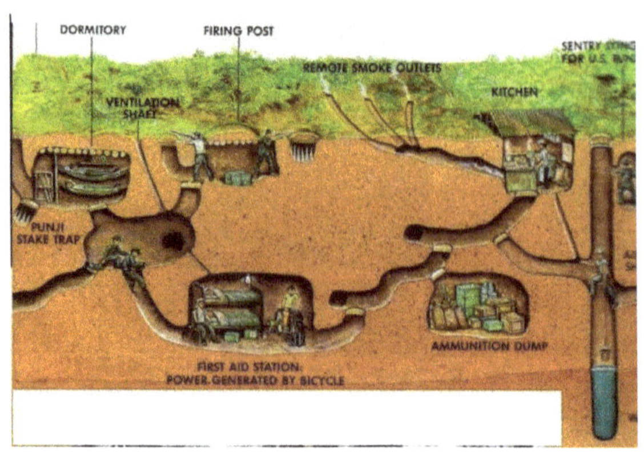

This drawing shows the complex network of the Cu Chi Tunnel system. The digging began in the mid to late 1940s, shortly after the surrender of the Japanese at the end of World War II. The tunnel system was dug to evade French army sweeps in the area at the onset of the 1st Indochina War. The tunnel system would continue as an ongoing project for the next 24 years, from 1945 to 1969. Its excavation ended only after North Vietnam capitulated to South Vietnamese and American forces along with their allies in 1969, and the 2nd Indochina War (Vietnam War) was over.

A Viet Cong soldier works on digging out a section of the Cu Chi Tunnel in 1946

The tunnels of Cu Chi are an immense network of connecting tunnels located in the Cu Chi District of Saigon, South Vietnam, and are part of a much larger network of tunnels that underlie much of the country.

64

The Cu Chi tunnels were the location of several military campaigns during the <u>Vietnam War</u>, and they served, along with the Ho Chi Minh trail, as the two most amazing feats of tactical engineering conducted by the North Vietnamese that very nearly won the war for them.

Indeed, it is theorized that had the Soviet Union and China not abandoned their support of North Vietnam in 1965, thus supplying the North with the war material needed to carry on the fight, these two factors would have very likely won the war for the North. The secret tunnels, which joined village to village and often passed beneath French and American bases in both wars, were not only fortifications for Viet Cong guerrillas, but were also the center of community life. Hidden beneath the destroyed villages were underground schools and public spaces where couples were married, and private places where lovers met were common. There were even theaters inside the tunnels where performers entertained with song and dance and traditional stories. But life in the tunnels was difficult. Air, food, and water were scarce, and the tunnels were infested with ants, poisonous centipedes, scorpions, spiders, snakes, and vermin. Most of the time, guerrillas would spend the day in the tunnels working or resting and come out only at night to scavenge for supplies, tend their crops, or engage the enemy in battle. Sometimes, during the 2nd Indochina War (Vietnam War), the Viet Cong would see periods of heavy bombing or American troop movement, and they would be forced to remain underground for many days at a time. Sickness was rampant among the people living in the tunnels, especially malaria, which was the second largest cause of death next to battle wounds. Almost everyone had intestinal parasites of significance. Only about 6,000 of the 16,000 soldiers who fought while being based in the tunnels survived the war. A captured Viet Cong report suggests that at any given time, half of a unit of the <u>People's Liberation Armed Forces</u> (PLAF) units had malaria and that *"one-hundred percent had intestinal parasites of significance."*

Throughout the course of the war, the tunnels in Ch Chi proved to be a source of frustration for the U.S. military in Saigon. The US and Australians tried a variety of methods to detect and infiltrate the tunnels, but all were met with failure. Large-scale ground operations involving tens of thousands of troops were launched. They ravaged rice paddies, bulldozed huge swathes of jungle, and villages were evacuated and razed. The Americans also sprayed chemical defoliants on the area aerially, and a few months later, ignited the tinder-dry vegetation with gasoline and napalm. By a strange twist of fate, the intense heat of the napalm interacted with the wet tropical air only to create cloudbursts that extinguished the fires. The Viet Cong guerrillas remained safe and sound inside their tunnels, at least for a time. Unable to win the battle with chemicals, the US army began sending men called *"tunnel rats"* down into the tunnels. Armed only with a gun, a knife, a flashlight, and a piece of string, these tunnel rats would enter a tunnel by themselves and travel inch by inch, cautiously looking ahead for booby traps. The job of a tunnel rat was fraught with immense dangers. The entrance holes in the ground were barely wide enough for the shoulders, let alone if the tunnel rat had any size to him at all. After a couple of meters of slipping and wriggling straight down, the narrow tunnel would take a U-turn back towards the surface, then twist again before heading off horizontally further. The light from the battery-powered lamp wasn't enough to pierce the darkness inside the tunnels, and there was no room to turn around and retreat. These conditions were so common that American soldiers began using the term *"Black Echo"* to describe the conditions within the tunnels.

The tunnel rats, who were often involved in underground firefights, sustained appallingly high casualty rates. The Americans then began using German shepherd dogs trained to use their keen sense of smell to locate trapdoors and guerrillas. The Viet Cong responded by washing themselves with American soap, which gave off a scent the canines identified as friendly. Captured US uniforms were put out in some areas of the tunnels to confuse the dogs further. Most importantly, the dogs were not able to spot booby traps. So many dogs were killed or maimed, and that led their horrified handlers to refuse to send the dogs into the tunnels. Finally, by the late 1960s, the Americans, who were now winning the war and had the enemy on the defensive, began carpet bombing Cu Chi with B-52 bombers. Once the bombers were relieved of their bombing missions over North Vietnam, they destroyed several portions of the tunnels along with everything else around the tunnels. By the end of the war, the 120-km-long complex of tunnels at Cu Chi had been effectively neutralized as a forward operations base for the Viet Cong, and had ultimately become a liability for them in terms of men and material lost, for it was clearly no longer a secret tunnel, as it had once been.

Operation Crimp (January 7-14, 1966)

An Australian sapper (left) inspects a Viet Cong tunnel discovered during Operation Crimp, in South Vietnam, January 1966. An Australian soldier (right) is pictured in a Viet Cong tunnel that was uncovered during the same operation.

In 1966, after four long years of frustration as to how the enemy managed to elude them during almost every engagement, the tunnels of Cu Chi were discovered, and it did not take long for U.S. officials to recognize the advantages that the Viet Cong held with the tunnels, and so they launched several major campaigns to search out and destroy the tunnel systems. Among the most important were Operation Crimp and Operation Cedar Falls. Operation Crimp (January 7-14, 1966), also known as the Battle of the Ho Bo Woods, was a joint US-Australian military operation during the Vietnam War, which took place 12 miles North of Cu Chi in the Binh Duong Province of South Vietnam. The operation targeted a key Viet Cong headquarters that was believed to be concealed underground, and involved two brigades under the command of the US 1st Infantry Division, including the 1st Battalion, Royal Australian Regiment (1 RAR), which was attached to the US 173rd Airborne Brigade. Heavy fighting resulted in significant casualties on both sides, but the combined American and Australian force was able to uncover an extensive tunnel network covering more than 120 miles. The operation was the largest allied military action mounted during the war in South Vietnam to that point, and the first fought at the division level.

Operation Crimp began on January 7, 1966, with B-52 bombers dropping 30-ton loads of high explosive onto the region of Cu Chi, effectively turning the once lush jungle into a pockmarked moonscape. Eight thousand troops from the U.S. 1st Infantry Division, 173rd Airborne Brigade Combat Team, and the 1st Battalion, Royal

<u>Australian Regiment</u> combed the region looking for any clues of <u>PLAF</u> activity.

Although the operation had netted some significant successes, the operation did not bring about the desired complete success hoped for by U.S. leaders. For instance, when troops found a tunnel, they would often underestimate its size. No one was usually sent in during this first tunnel engagement to search the tunnels, as it was so hazardous. Within the tunnels, they were often rigged with explosive <u>booby traps</u> or <u>punji stick</u> pits.

The two most common responses by the Americans and Australians in dealing with a tunnel opening would be to flush the entrance with gas, water, or hot tar to force the Viet Cong soldiers into the open or to toss a few grenades down the hole and *"crimp"* off the opening. Those approaches proved ineffective because of the design of the tunnels and the strategic use of trap doors and air filtration systems.

A trap door on the jungle floor (left) leads down into the Cu Chi tunnels. Closed and camouflaged, it is almost undetectable. The camouflaged trap door (right), now open, shows just how the enemy manages to melt away from a battle as though they had never been there. Indeed, while the South Vietnamese or its allies may control the ground above, the ground below can still be fully occupied by a full troop of enemy forces.

An American M-113 Armored Assault Vehicle (left) and a US 105 mm Howitzer (right) are pictured providing search and destroy and fire support to the US 173rd Airborne Brigade on the final day of Operation Crimp, January 1966, in what later became known as the Battle of the Ho Bo Woods.

Alexander "Sandy" MacGregor

(1940-****)

Robert "Bob" Bowtell

(1932-1966)

However, an Australian specialist engineering troop, 3 Field Troop, Royal Australian Engineers, under the command of Captain <u>Alexander "Sandy" MacGregor</u> (later Colonel), ventured into the tunnels, which they searched exhaustively for four days. Later, he would report… *"I found ammunition, radio equipment, medical supplies, food, and signs of a considerable Viet Cong presence."*

One of their sappers, Corporal Robert *"Bob"* Bowtell, died when he became trapped in a tunnel that turned out to be a dead end. However, the Australians pressed on and revealed for the first time the immense military significance of the tunnels. At an international press conference in <u>Saigon</u> shortly after Operation Crimp, MacGregor referred to his men as *"tunnel ferrets."* An American journalist who had never heard of ferrets used the term *"tunnel rats,"* and it stuck. After his troop's discoveries in Cu Chi, MacGregor was awarded a <u>Military Cross</u>.

Ellis W. *"Butch"* Williamson

(1918-2007)

From its mistakes and the Australians' discoveries, the U.S. command realized that it needed a new way to approach the dilemma of the tunnels. A general order was issued by General Williamson, the Allied Forces Commander in South Vietnam, to all Allied forces that tunnels had to be properly searched whenever they were discovered. It began training an elite group of volunteers in the art of tunnel warfare, armed only with a handgun, a knife, a flashlight, and a piece of string. The specialists, commonly known as *"tunnel rats"*, would enter a tunnel by themselves and travel inch by inch, cautiously looking ahead for booby traps or cornered PLAF. There was no real doctrine for the approach, and despite some very hard work in some sectors of the Army and the Military Assistance Command, Vietnam, to provide some sort of training and resources, it was primarily a new approach that the units trained, equipped, and planned for themselves.

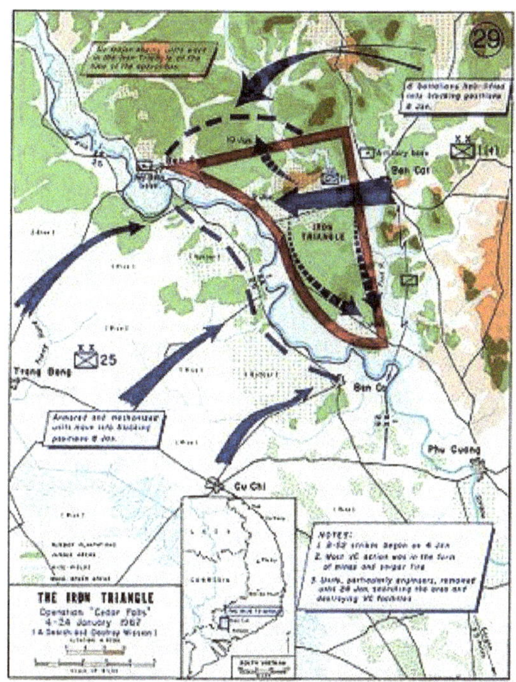

Map of Operation Cedar Falls, (The Iron Triangle) January 8-27, 1967

<u>Operation Cedar Falls</u> (January 8-27, 1967)

Operation Cedar Falls was a military operation of the Vietnam War conducted primarily by US forces that took place from 8 to 26 January 1967. The aim of the massive search-and-destroy operation was to eradicate the so-called *"Iron Triangle"*, an area northwest of Saigon that had become a major stronghold of the Viet Cong (VC).

It was the largest American ground operation of the Vietnam War to date; two Army divisions, one infantry and one paratrooper brigade, and one armored cavalry regiment participated in the operation. Altogether, it involved 30,000 US and South Vietnamese troops. The VC, however, chose to evade the massive military force by fleeing across the border to <u>Cambodia</u> by way of the Ho Chi Minh trail or by hiding in a complex system of tunnels. Still, the Allied forces uncovered and destroyed some of the tunnel complexes as well as large stockpiles of VC supplies.

In an attempt at the permanent destruction of the Iron Triangle as a VC stronghold, Operation Cedar Falls also entailed the complete deportation of the region's civilian population to so-called New Life Villages, with the destruction of their homes and the defoliation of whole areas.

Following this, the area was declared a <u>free-fire zone</u>, and adults who were found in the zone following deportations were considered "enemy combatants" afterward. Most senior officers involved in planning and executing the operation later evaluated it as a success. Despite the revamped effort at fighting the enemy on their own terms, however, U.S. operations remained insufficient at eliminating the tunnels completely.

<u>William Childs Westmoreland</u>

(1914-2005)

On January 18, 1967, General <u>William Westmoreland</u> decided to use the newly formed tunnel rats from the 1st Battalion, <u>5th Infantry Regiment</u>, <u>25th Infantry Division</u>. They uncovered the Viet Cong district headquarters of Cu Chi, containing half a million documents concerning all types of military strategy. Among the documents were maps of U.S. bases, detailed accounts of PLAF movement from <u>Cambodia</u> into Vietnam, and lists of political sympathizers.

A fellow American soldier helps a *"tunnel rat"* soldier out of a tunnel after a successful mission during Operation Cedar Falls in South Vietnam, January 1967.

Aggravated with the continued ability of the enemy to cross into Cambodia and Laos along the Ho Chi Minh trail to what amounted to *"safe havens"* in those neutral countries for them, from total defeat or capture, General Westmoreland gets President Nixon's approval, along with Congress' approval, to begin bombing the trail and sending troops in pursuit after the retreating enemy forces whenever they attempt this. Once the allowance for this was agreed upon by the governments of these two countries, the operations began across the borders of both countries in earnest. This *"pursue-and-hit"* strategy continues for the next two years.

The Tet Offensive (January 29 - February 25, 1968)

After being freed from constant bombing runs over North Vietnam and the enemy capitol of Hanoi, and the successful American invasion was underway throughout the North, this American B-52 bomber and others, are pictured carpet bombing the tunnels of Cu Chi and the rest of the Iron Triangle on January 31, 1968.

By January 29, 1968, many of the B-52s were freed from bombing North Vietnam and started *"carpet bombing"* Cu Chi and the rest of the Iron Triangle, along with the enemy forces still moving along the trail or still trying to use the two countries of Laos and Cambodia as safe havens along the Ho Chi Minh trail. Towards the end of the war, the tunnels were so heavily bombed that some portions actually caved in, and other sections became completely exposed.

Also on January 29, 1968, in accordance with South Vietnam's wishes on this day in which to launch the coordinated attacks that was planned for the Vietnamese Lunar New Year, (known as Tet) which was a series of seven coordinated attacks that spanned three countries, the Tet Offensive, as it would later be called, turned out to be a day that marked the beginning of the end for the North. While the United States had balked at South Vietnam's willingness to break the truce that had been called by both sides to honor the Tet Holiday, the U.S. commanders, with President Nixon's blessing to do so, had decided to launch the attacks due to the fact that the audacious boldness of the plan was simply breathtaking. The South Vietnamese figured that the enemy would never expect it and maybe would have their guard down when it all started. With the planned attacks, the U.S. had finally decided to branch out, while they left the South Vietnamese and the other foreign allied forces that were *"in country"* to continue to fight the beleaguered and materially starved enemy forces in Laos, Cambodia and South Vietnam, to effectively close the trail all along its length, for the U.S. had all but completely ended the enemies ground to air threat along the trail, the United States looked North. Having destroyed most of North Vietnam's ability to be much of a threat to its war planes that now roamed to skies over the North with impunity, for the North had extinguished virtually all of its supply of Sam (Surface to Air Missiles) and most of its anti-aircraft ammunition as well as its heavy automatic weapons ammunition, was forced to fight primarily a ground war to try and counter the invasion that came, just as their forces along the trail were having to do as well.

The South Vietnamese Air Force continued the pressure along with American B-52 bombers on the Ho Chi Minh trail as they began their own pincer movement, first cutting off the trail at the North Vietnamese/Laotian border with American helicopter borne troops that were inserted at the border to drive South through Laos as more chopper borne troops landed at the South Vietnamese/Cambodian border and drove North, their objective was to conduct a pincer movement that forced the enemy troops caught along the trail in an ever diminishing pocket that continued to be bombed by the planes above, with these troops in those two countries neutralized even before they reached South Vietnam, then the mopping up phase could begin in South Vietnam for what was left of them along with their Communist sympathizers, both military and civilian.

And also on January 29, 1968, while the South Vietnamese Army, along with their Marine and Ranger units and other allies, began their three-pronged ground and air attack in Laos, Cambodia, and South Vietnam. The United States launches the largest American ground, air, and sea operation of the Vietnam War, and it proved to be even larger than Operation Cedar Falls. A four pronged air, sea and ground assault that saw chopper borne U.S. Army and Ranger unit troops landed on the Laotian/North Vietnamese border with orders to move through the Nape Pass North and cut off any retreating enemy forces that may decide to head that way and link up with their forces in Laos and or Cambodia should they think that those forces were not being threatened. They then dropped more chopper-borne U.S. Army and Green Beret troops along the area bordering the Chinese/North Vietnamese border in the villages of Hai Ninh, Lang Son, Cao Bang, Dong Van, Ha Giang, Lao Cai, and the Black River Valley, West/Northwest of Lai Chau. They did this to counter any enemy troops that might try to retreat into China and to discourage China from attempting to re-enter the fray in the form of actual ground troops to try and save their beleaguered neighbors, as they had done with a surprise attack across the border in North and South Korea during that war. Meanwhile, U.S. Marines, carefully making their way through the maze of minds that had been laid in the harbor back in 1962, made an amphibious landing at the Port of Haiphong and made their way towards Hanoi, and U.S. Army and Marines crossed the demilitarized zone and the international border with North and South Vietnam and proceeded north to block possible enemy retreats from the Ho Chi

Minh trail through the Ban Karai and the Mu Gia passes as well. As an added precaution, the U.S. Army conducted Paratrooper drops in 17 towns and villages all across the Democratic Republic of North Vietnam. Only the villages and cities of Haiphong, Hanoi, and those along the border of China did not receive Paratroopers, for they were receiving chopper-borne troops. In short, every town and village in North Vietnam was to receive a visit by U.S. forces this day. The American phase of this seven coordinated attacks in three nations, had been perhaps the most audacious of the entire campaign, for it included a *"blanket attack"* of the entire country of North Vietnam, involving every town and village known in the country, to be hit at the same time, thus giving the enemy no time to regroup or retreat from the surprise offensive. It was the largest land, air, and sea operation since the enormous attacks conducted during the Normandy Invasion, known as D-Day, back on June 6, 1944, during World War II, or the Inchon Invasion during the Korean War.

Even with this massive effort during the Tet Offensive, for the offensive had been designed to end the war with one huge and massive sweeping effort, and while it did clearly knock the wind out of the proverbial sails of the North Vietnamese in their resolve to continue the war, the war still dragged on for another painstaking year, two months and nine days until its end on April 9, 1969.

A Changing of the Guard (The 1968 Presidential Election)

Like President Franklin D. Roosevelt towards the close of World War II, President Richard M. Nixon would not be in the White House when the end of the Vietnam War had finally come. Unlike Roosevelt, Nixon would still be alive at the end of the Vietnam War, for Roosevelt had died on April 12, 1945, less than a month before Victory in Europe was won on May 8th with Germany's surrender. It would be left to Harry S. Truman, Roosevelt's Vice-President, to take up the reigns and lead the Allied war to final Victory in the Pacific, with that, World War II had fully ended on September 2, 1945. Now, a new president would have to lead the war effort in the Pacific to its ultimate victorious end. Truman, who knew full well that the victory won in Europe had already been a virtual win by Roosevelt in not only Europe but the entire war, however, he knew he was merely conducting the "mop-up" operations that finally did end the war under his watch. Likewise, Nelson Aldrich Rockefeller also knew that he too had been left with the "mop up" operations that would finally see the end of the Vietnam War as well, for all knew that although Rockefeller was an important part in seeing the war to its final victory, it was Nixon and his leadership, that had been so instrumental in helping to reach that ultimate victorious outcome. Nixon was reaching the end of his second and final four-year term in office as President, and under the Twenty-Second Amendment of the Constitution of the United States, he was ineligible to run for a third term. Indeed, he had held the office of Vice-President for two consecutive terms under President Dwight D. Eisenhower, and then went on to serve two consecutive terms as President as well, thus bringing his time in the White House to four consecutive terms, 16 years, holding both of those Executive seats of power. The 1968 Presidential election would see Nixon's Vice-President, who himself had held two consecutive four-year terms as Vice-President, try to repeat what Nixon had done. He would go on to run for the highest office in the land so he could carry on Nixon's plans for ending the war in Southeast Asia, then he could get down to the business of what was near and dear to his heart, his plans for social welfare for his fellow countrymen at home. He would choose Raymond P. Shafer, Governor of Pennsylvania, as his running mate. He and Shaffer would go on to win the election against Governor George Corley Wallace Jr. of Alabama and retired four-star general Curtis LeMay of California.

Raymond Philip Shafer

(1917-2006)

Curtis Emerson LeMay

(1906-1990)

1968 United States Presidential Election

← 1964 **November 5, 1968** 1972 →

	Nelson A. Rockefeller	George C. Wallace
Nominee	**Nelson A. Rockefeller**	George C. Wallace
Party	Republican	Democratic
Home state	New York	Alabama
Running mate	**Raymond P. Shafer**	Curtis LeMay
Electoral vote	**301**	237
States carried	**32**	18 + DC
Popular vote	**31,783,783**	41,172,957
Percentage	**43.4%**	56.2%

Rockefeller/Shaffer '68

538 members of the <u>Electoral College</u>

270 electoral votes needed to win

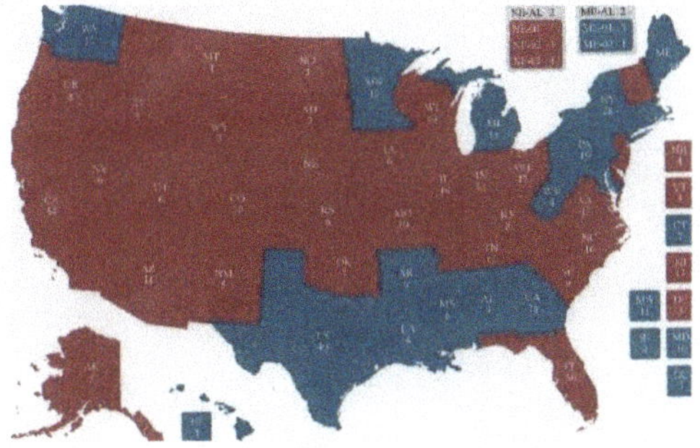

Presidential Election Results

Red denotes states won by Rockefeller/Shafer, and Blue denotes states won by Wallace/LeMay.

Note: 32 states were carried by the Rockefeller/Shafer ticket, and 18 states and the District of Columbia (DC) were carried by the Wallace/LeMay ticket.

Note: In this election, the people of the United States seemed to get over their dismay in the District of Columbia with their unwillingness to vote for the Wallace/Thurmond ticket in the previous election of '64, for that year saw a historical shift in DC, and the district overwhelmingly voted Republican. This year, however, the Wallace/LeMay ticket enjoyed a much larger turnout, and DC had finally come back to its roots and overwhelmingly voted for the Democratic ticket, but it proved useless in the long run as the Rockefeller/Shafer ticket would ultimately prevail. Many political experts theorized that if Wallace had chosen LeMay in '64 instead of Thurmond, he might have enjoyed a much larger turnout, and even if he had still lost in '64, the turnout in '68 might have been larger than it was, thus causing him to win the '68 election. Indeed, Wallace had won the popular vote by some 9,389,174 votes over Rockefeller, but lost the Electoral vote by some 64 votes. His overall percentage over Rockefeller was 12.8%. It was election numbers like these that prompted many people in and out of government to begin calling for the abolishment of the Electoral College in favor of the popular vote alone, an outcome that has yet to be realized.

President Before Election	**Elected President**
Richard Milhous Nixon	Nelson Aldrich Rockefeller
Republican	Republican

Earl Warren

(1891-1974)

Chief Justice of the Supreme Court Earl Warren administers the oath of office during the Inauguration of President-Elect Nelson Aldrich Rockefeller as the 36th President of the United States on the East Portico of the US. Capitol on Monday, January 20, 1969. This was the 46th inauguration and marked the first of two terms that he would hold in office.

The Siege of Hanoi (March 1 - April 4, 1969)

The bulk of the American forces, after having secured the whole of North Vietnam, and leaving relief forces to maintain the hold on the country's recently acquired territory as well as the towns and cities left in its wake, made their final march to Hanoi and proceeded to surround the embattled city. The Siege of Hanoi began on March 1, 1969, and would finally be over after 35 days of intense artillery shelling, which included air and sea bombardment as well. The American forces dug in all around the city and simply waited to see if the enemy would capitulate after all the bombardment, or would they insist on a bitter hand-to-hand conflict within the ruins of the city, for a cause that was clearly lost for them. The answer to this question finally came in the early morning hours of April 9, 1969, when the Americans began seeing enemy troops all over the beleaguered city, laying down their weapons and hoisting the white flags of surrender.

American tanks (left) and troops (right) make their way ever closer to the center of Hanoi, seeking to capture the Presidential Palace, the Politburo, and the Hanoi Citadel. If these places of Communist government can be captured, the city is sure to fall, thus forcing the leaders of Hanoi to finally admit defeat and seek surrender terms.

Fierce fighting ensues as the American forces reach the city's center (left). When the city is secured and the surrender becomes complete, the photo (right) shows the extent of how very little of the city remains untouched by the ravages of war.

After the surrender, it took days to gather all the dead that still littered the streets of Hanoi (left), and while the city and country was secured, there were still hold outs that refused to surrender even after having received orders to do so by Ho Chi Minh himself, as seen here in the photo where Marines are attempting to flush out some of the hold outs located in the rubble just outside the city (right).

A Marine stands guard over a captured enemy holdout (left), one of two that had been captured in a pile of rubble just outside the city, and his comrade is being interrogated while he waits his turn to be questioned. It does not take long for the civilian population of the city to begin their rummaging amongst the rubble of their war-torn city (right), in a vain quest to find anything of value that may have survived the relentless bombing of the city. This photo shows in graphic detail the harsh realities of war and the consequences of blindly following a regime bent on nothing but war and the subjugation of others. By doing so, they ended up receiving the very thing they had sought to force on the people of South Vietnam.

Chapter Ten

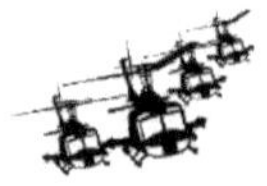

The End Finally Comes (1969)

At long last, the forces of North Vietnam, after having suffered the fall of every one of its other towns and villages in the country, had all retreated to Hanoi for a last-ditch effort to try and stave off the inevitable there, for the rest of the country was firmly in American hands. In Laos and Cambodia, the enemy forces there had put up a valiant fight after being backed into an area no more than ten miles wide from any direction within a complete circle, from the forces that pushed South from the Laotian/North Vietnamese border, and the forces that pushed North from the Cambodian/ South Vietnamese border, finally trapping the embattled enemy forces in Laos. With the mopping up operations in South Vietnam completed, more forces were heading west to help mop up the enemy forces that were still there in Laos, for Cambodia, as was South Vietnam, was also free of the enemy forces there as well. The enemy forces in Laos surrendered in the field on April 1, 1969, and once Hanoi, already under siege itself, was finally contacted by the ranking North Vietnamese commander, General Hoàng Văn Thái, who had surrendered, and had arrived at the prisoner of war camp in Saigon on April 2, 1969; it took the North Vietnamese Politburo in Hanoi two days to convince Ho Chi Minh to finally sue for peace before Hanoi was forced to surrender in disgrace as well, like the commander in Laos had done.

General Hoàng Văn Thái

(1915-1986)

From 1967 to 1969, Thái was assigned to the South to command the North Vietnamese and Viet Cong forces there; he was made Commander of the People's Liberation Armed Forces (PLAF) and Deputy Secretary of the Central Executive Committee of the People's Revolutionary Party. The US army called him a *"3-legged tiger"* because he was the highest-ranking Northern commander in the South during the war years. After the war, he immigrated to China and is buried in Beijing, the country's capital.

Minh had hoped that his forces in the South would be able to break through and come to the aid of his besieged city, but when he had heard of his forces there surrendering, he was crestfallen. He had called for his troops to lay down their arms on April 4, 1969, at daylight; by midday, the city was swarming with U.S. troops. When some of the occupying troops made their way to the Hanoi Citadel, General Võ Nguyên Giáp, who was born on August 25, 1911, initially refused to give up his command post, but seeing the amount of American forces waiting just outside his office, and having no forces himself to resist with, he finally sees the hopelessness of further resistance, and walked out to give himself up. After the war, Giáp immigrated to North Korea, where he lived out his retirement in exile, passing away on October 4, 2013, at the age of 102. His body, upon approval from the government in Saigon, is returned to Nixon City (formally Hanoi), and is buried at his former home province of <u>Quang Binh</u> with full military honors conducted by former North Vietnamese soldiers dressed in full dress uniforms, and given a 21 gun salute, firing with blanks in the same fashion that Ho Chi Minh's funeral had been conducted back in 1969.

Võ Nguyên Giáp   Fredrick C. Weyand

(1911-2013)   (1916-2010)

General Võ Nguyên Giáp (left) was the Military Minister of the Democratic Republic of Vietnam. He entertained the thought of resisting American forces as they stood outside his Hanoi Citadel headquarters after Hanoi fell to the Americans on April 4, 1969, but thought better of it when he realized the futility of further resistance. Lieutenant General Frederick Weyand (right) was appointed the Commander of U.S. forces in what was now being called Zero Corps, which included the Capital Military District of Hanoi and the whole of occupied North Vietnam after the country's fall and occupation.

Weyand received the Surrender of Hanoi from General Giáp after Minh's general call for all North Vietnamese forces to lay down their arms and cease hostilities. Weyand, a former intelligence officer, was suspicious however of the pattern of Communist activities that was still prevalent in the area of his responsibility and notified General Westmoreland of his concerns on April 28, 1969, and suggested that a roundup of all suspected Communist who were still roaming the country in secret be detained until they could be made to swear allegiance to the victorious Republic of Vietnam or leave Southeast Asia and migrate to another country of their choosing. Westmoreland agreed with his estimate and ordered 15 U.S. battalions to redeploy from positions in the South near the Cambodian border to the outskirts of Hanoi.

This redeployment may have been one of the most critical tactical decisions of the post-war occupation, for it demonstrated to the people of the former Communist country that their ideology of Socialism and Communist beliefs would not be tolerated in the occupied country.

The <u>Hanoi Citadel</u> was the military headquarters of General Giáp during the war, from 1962 to 1969.

While the occupation of the city resumed, Ho was flown to Japan to await the trip to Switzerland, to meet with the officials of all the victorious allied forces there at the Bern Peace Conference. Ho, an old man by this time and already in ill health, looked positively ancient as he entered the chamber hall in Bern, Switzerland, on April 9, 1969. The meeting was purely for the purpose of signing the agreements that had been hammered out the previous day. When the treaty was signed, the Democratic Republic of North Vietnam, the country he had declared independent back in 1945 and had helped to found after the Japanese surrender at the end of World War II, had ceased to exist. His people had fought three wars, as a Revolutionary Army set out to win its independence from their Japanese occupiers, to a fledging Communist country that sought to retain what it had won against the Japanese with a war against the French to resist a return to pre World War II colonial rule by France in the 1st Indochina War, to its ultimate demise in the 2nd Indochina War (The Vietnam War) by the Republic of South Vietnam and its allies.

The treaty (known as the Treaty of Bern), called for the elimination of the government in Hanoi and for the former countries citizens to swear allegiance to the Republic of Vietnam (South Vietnam) and its ruling government in Saigon, or leave Southeast Asia for whatever country they wish to immigrate to if that country will accept them, thus never returning to Southeast Asia unless they were prepared to pledge allegiance when they did return. When all was said and done, most of the hard line Communist believers reluctantly immigrated to either China or the Soviet Union, with a few going to Cuba or to North Korea, but it was a hard choice for many, for they viewed each of these countries as having stabbed their former country in the back at the hour of its greatest need, for they would be required to swear allegiance to these countries, and that came hard to them. Many of the less faithful of the Communist ideology, or those who did not believe in the Communist ideology at all, but had no choice in the matter as to what government ruled their country, chose to stay in what was even now being referred to as simply the Republic of Vietnam, thus dropping the phrase South Vietnam, even though they still lived in the North. In time, this name would be changed as the country voted to rename itself the United Republic of Vietnam.

1972 United States Presidential Election

    November 7, 1972

	Nelson A. Rockefeller	George McGovern
Nominee	**Nelson A. Rockefeller**	George McGovern
Party	Republican	Democratic
Home state	New York	South Dakota
Running mate	**Raymond P. Shafer**	Robert S. Shriver Jr.
Electoral vote	**502**	17
States carried	**49**	1 + DC
Popular vote	**47,168,710**	29,173,222
Percentage	**60.7%**	37.5%

Rockefeller/Shaffer '72

538 members of the <u>Electoral College</u>
270 electoral votes needed to win

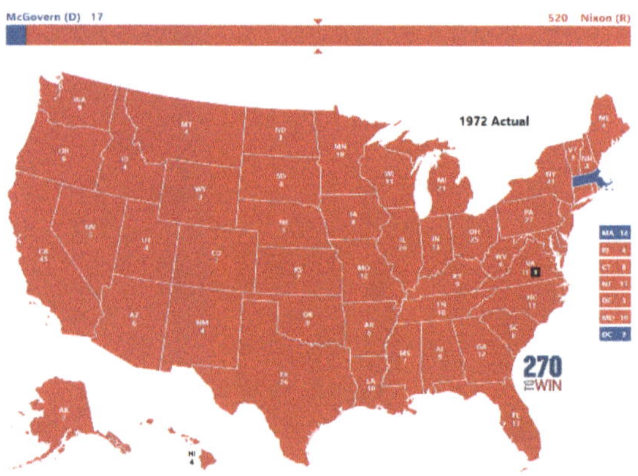

Presidential Election Results

Red denotes states won by Rockefeller/Shafer, and Blue denotes states won by McGovern/Shriver.

Emphasizing a good economy and his successes in foreign affairs (especially finishing the war by winning it in Vietnam after President Nixon had begun that win during his two terms in office), President Rockefeller won his re-election in a massive landslide (with an even higher proportion than in 1964, when Nixon had won, overwhelmingly defeating George Wallace). Rockefeller wins the election with a 23.2% margin of victory in the popular vote, the forth largest margin in Presidential Election history. He received almost 18 million more votes than McGovern, the widest margin of any U.S. Presidential Election.

<table>
<tr><td align="center">President Before Election</td><td align="center">Elected President</td></tr>
<tr><td align="center">Nelson Aldrich Rockefeller
Republican</td><td align="center">Nelson Aldrich Rockefeller
Republican</td></tr>
</table>

A whopping 49 states were carried by the Rockefeller/Shafer ticket, and only 1 state and the District of Columbia (DC) were carried by the McGovern/Shriver ticket. This resulted in the Rockefeller/Shafer ticket receiving 520 electoral votes in the Electoral College, and the McGovern/Shriver ticket receiving only 17 electoral votes. Without a doubt, the 1972 election would go down as the most one-sided election in U.S. Presidential Election history, and would likely not be repeated or surpassed for perhaps generations to come.

John Hospers

(1918-2011)

Theodora Nathalie "Tonie" Nathan

(1923-2014)

Roger Lea MacBride

(1929-1995)

One Virginia faithless elector vote was won by the Hospers/Nathan Libertarian Party ticket. John Hospers became the first presidential candidate of the new Libertarian Party and was the only minor party candidate to receive an electoral vote in the 1972 U.S. Presidential Election. Hospers would go on to pick Tonie Nathan as his Vice-Presidential running mate; the one electoral vote that he and Nathan would win was from the faithless elector Roger MacBride, a Republican from Virginia, resulting in Nathan becoming the first woman and the first Jew to receive an electoral vote in a United States Presidential Election.

Chief Justice of the Supreme Court Warren E. Burger administers the oath of office during the 2nd Inauguration of President Nelson Aldrich Rockefeller as the 36th President of the United States on the West Front of the U.S. Capitol on Saturday, January 20, 1973. This was the 47th inauguration and marked the 2nd of two terms that he would hold in office after he won the 1972 election, defeating Democratic Senator George McGovern and his Vice-Presidential running mate, U.S. Ambassador to France Robert S. Shriver Jr. After his two terms in office, he returned to New York and retired from public service.

Warren E. Burger

(1907-1995)

George McGovern	Robert Shriver Jr.	Jimmy Carter	Walter Mondale	Albert "Al" Gore Jr.
(1922-2012)	(1915-2011)	(1928-2021)	(1928-2021)	(1948-****)

Note: In the 1976 Presidential Election, after 24 years of Republican rule in the White House, the people of the United States elect Democratic Governor of Georgia James Earl (Jimmy) Carter and his running mate Walter Fredrick (Fritz) Mondale of Minnesota as his Vice-President, this makes Carter the 37th President, but when the 1980 election rolls around, the people have had enough of Democratic rule after just four years. They elect Republican Governor of California Ronald Wilson "Dutch" Reagan as the 38th President and his running mate George Herbert Walker Bush of Texas as his Vice-President, and the Reagan Revolution begins, and although this stint of Republican rule last for only twelve years with the four years Bush serves as the 39th President, the next Democrat, William Jefferson "Bill" Clinton of Arkansas and his running mate Albert Arnold "Al" Gore Jr. of Tennessee as his Vice-President, see election to the White House, this makes Clinton the 40th President. In retrospect, however, these twelve years during the Reagan/Bush administrations seem to outshine even all of the 24 years of the Eisenhower, Nixon, and Rockefeller administrations combined.

Epilogue

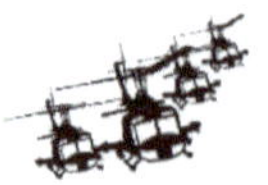

The United Republic of Vietnam (1976-Present)

(1890-Present)

National Flag of the United Republic of Vietnam

Thanh Thai

(1879-1954)

Bao Dai

(1913-1997)

Le Van De

(1906-1966)

The flag was originally inspired by <u>Emperor</u> <u>Thanh Thai</u> in 1890, and was revived by <u>Le Van De</u> and re-adopted by Emperor Bao Dai in 1948. The flag consists of a yellow field and three horizontal red stripes and can be explained as either symbolizing the unifying blood running through northern, central, and southern Vietnam, or as representing the symbol for "South" (as in, South from <u>China</u> (Vietnam itself) and also Nam meaning South), in <u>Daoist</u> <u>trigrams</u>. Another explanation for the strips is that they represent freedom, democracy, and equality; the three red strips also represent the blood that was lost during the struggle for independence. At one time, it was referred to as the Yellow Banner or Yellow Flag for short, with the yellow background representing the skin tone of the Vietnamese people. The flag is known today as the Heritage and Freedom Flag, thus symbolizing the heritage of the republic and the freedom of the people.

(1890-Present)

National Emblem of the United Republic of Vietnam

The meanings for the National Emblem are the same as the National flag as well.

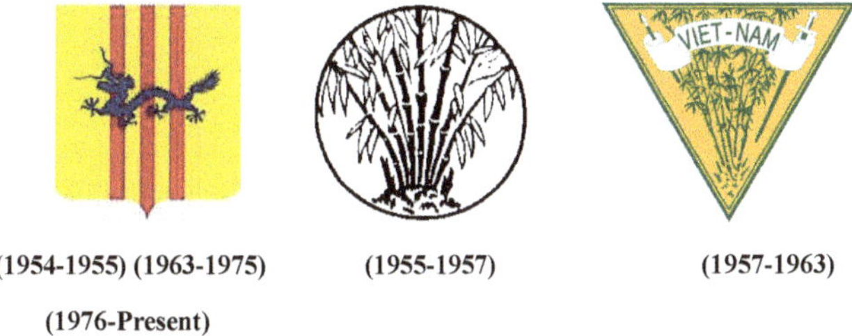

(1954-1955) (1963-1975)   (1955-1957)   (1957-1963)

(1976-Present)

National Coat of Arms for the United Republic of Vietnam

The 1st Coat of arms shown here served from 1954 to 1955, when it was changed to the 2nd Coat of Arms shown, this coat served from 1955 to 1957 until it was changed yet again to the 3rd Coat of Arms, and this coat served from 1957 to 1963. These designs reflect how indecisive and ever-changing the Ngo Dinh Diem government was during its eight years in power, and ultimately how unreliable President Diem was himself. After Diem was removed from power, Duong Van Minh became the country's President, and he brought the original design back as the National Coat of Arms from 1963 to 1975. The design of the Coat of Arms and the Presidential flag remained in limbo until they were both voted on in 1976 by the Vietnamese Congress, where they both became the permanent Coat of Arms and Presidential flag of the United Republic of Vietnam.

(1976-Present)

National Military Flag of the United Republic of Vietnam

While there are different flags for each branch of the military of the United Republic of Vietnam, the National Military Flag represents all of the military branches as a whole.

(1955-1963)   (1976-Present)

The Presidential Standard of the Republic of Vietnam under the Ngo Dinh Diem government (left), where the inscription means *"Duty and Sacrifice,"* and the Presidential Standard of the President of the United Republic of Vietnam as Supreme Commander of the <u>Military Forces</u> (right). After the war was won, this latter flag was adopted as the permanent standard for the President of the United Republic of Vietnam in 1976, and remains so to this present day. (Note: From 1963 to 1976, there was no Presidential flag adopted by the Duong Van Minh administration. The new design, above right, would finally be adopted by the Vietnamese Congress on the country's 7th annual independence celebration known as *"Freedom Day"* on April 9, 1976. The new National Military Flag design, above center, would also be adopted on this day.)

Outline Map of the United Republic of Vietnam

The United Republic of Vietnam National Anthem

Call to the Citizens

On Citizens! Our country has reached the day of liberation. Of one heart we go forth, sacrificing ourselves with no regrets. For the future of the people, advance into battle; let us make this land eternally strong. Should our bodies be left on the battlefields, the nation will be avenged with our crimson blood.

In troublesome times, the Race will be rescued; we, the People, remain resolute in our hearts and minds. Courageously we will fight such that everywhere, the glory of the Vietnamese forever resounds!

Oh citizens! Hasten to offer yourselves under the flag! Oh citizens! Hasten to make this land, escape from destruction, and bask our Race in glory. Be forever worthy of the descendants of Lac Hong descendants!

The National Banner, the National Emblem, and the National Anthem show a proud history of this young country known as the United Republic of Vietnam. Against all the odds, they managed to prevail. At the very onset of its birth, they were invaded by enemy forces from without and within, wholly bent on one course, the total destruction of their young republic, and the complete subjugation of its people. Many mistakes had been made during the course of the struggle they had to endure in order for them to have the right of self-government and freedom from an oppression that they did not deserve, but many other decisions had been the right ones as well.

The fight had been long and hard, lasting some 24 years from 1945, shortly after the surrender of Japan at the end of World War II, to 1969, when victory was finally won, and independence was achieved. Thanks to the United States; and to the tenacity of President Richard M. Nixon, who had refused to give up on the fledging young republic, that victory would not have been possible, and the people of the United Republic of Vietnam knew that all to well.

Former President Richard Milhous Nixon, standing at the base of the monument dedicated to him in downtown Saigon, located at "Hero's Square" on April 9, 1980, during the country's 11th independence holiday known as *"Freedom Day."* He is hailed as the *"Savior of Southeast Asia"* in the United States and as the *"Father of the Republic"* in the United Republic of Vietnam.

In 1980, to honor the man and the country who had made their independence possible, the people of the United Republic of Vietnam showed their remembrance with the placement of a huge statue, standing some thirty feet high with a ring of five United States flags lined behind the statue in a half moon configuration, this monument was unveiled on the anniversary of the end of the war, April 9 1969, known as Freedom Day. The monument was constructed right in the middle of Saigon, the nation's capital, and it had taken the past 11 years to have the statue designed and placed at the new site that had been constructed for it. Indeed, it stood right in front of the country's capital building, which served as the legislative seat of the country's government. It was surrounded by many other statues of some of the country's notable heroes of the war, and the area where the statues stood was known as "Heroes' *Square.* " This statue, however, stood far taller and larger than the other statues, for the person this statue honored was considered by the people of the United Republic of Vietnam as the *"Father of the Republic."*

The person in question had never been a citizen of the United Republic of Vietnam, and had not helped to establish the country at its birth, but he was considered the Father of the Republic by the people because, had he not helped the republic during its hour of greatest need, there would be no republic, and they knew it.

The day of the unveiling had been unseasonably cool for weather in Saigon, the temperature peaked at just 79 degrees, far lower than the typical 90 to 97 degrees for this time of the year in the city, but the dignitaries that began to gather from all over the world from the many hotels and motels throughout the city, to attend the unveiling ceremony, certainly wasn't going to complain.

They came from many of the young republics' allied countries, some of which had also helped during the war, and they considered this ceremony worthy of their time. The ceremony, however, could not start until its guest of honor had arrived, and he was due to do just that at any moment.

The limousine carrying the honored guest finally rolled into view. It came to a stop about half a city block from where everyone was gathered. The driver of the limo exited the vehicle and made his way to the other side of the car, and opened the door to let the guest out. As the man rose to his full height, a height that was already beginning to show a slightly hunched appearance due to his age, a nearby band from the Vietnamese Marine Corps began playing *"Hail to the Chief."*

Richard M. Nixon smiled as he acknowledged the band and their flawless performance of the song honoring his position as a former

President of the United States. He began to wave to the gathered crowd of civilians that were kept behind crowd control fences, who had gathered to catch a glimpse of the revered man as he made his way to the podium that he was being directed to. There, a seat of honor was placed for him at the center of the podium just behind and to the right of the lectern so that the dignitaries gathered could see the man as they listened to other guest speakers that made their speeches just before the unveiling was to occur, once that was done, Nixon would then give his acceptance speech of the honor being bestowed upon him.

Finally, the preliminary speeches had all been completed, and all rose to their feet as the unveiling commenced. The crowd, both dignitaries and civilians alike, gave a collective gasp as their eyes gazed upon the colossal figure of a man, standing straight and tall and seeming to gesture with his slightly upraised right hand to someone only he could see, as his left hand rested on a book sitting by a small table. It was a perfect likeness of the man who was the guest of honor. Nixon began to lightly weep as the gravity of the moment began to truly sink into him, for to him, this was the high-water mark to a long and storied political career. At home, he had been hailed as the *"Savior of Southeast Asia,"* and honored already with smaller statues, as well as schools, streets, and bridges being named in his honor all across the United States, and now this honor had been simply overwhelming for him. Not a man to lose his emotions easily, he simply couldn't stop himself as he gazed at the massive monument. Finally, he managed to get a hold of himself as he was being directed to say a few words. He had had a prepared speech, but he knew now that it would be wholly inadequate for this occasion. Unlike his usual nature, when it came to making speeches, he decided to simply speak from the heart, for an honor of this magnitude demanded nothing less.

He walked to the lectern and looked out over the crowd as he put away his handkerchief into his pocket. He gazed out over the crowd and, slightly tilting towards the array of microphones before him, he said:

"To the august assembly here today, gathered from this great republic, the United Republic of Vietnam, and of those of you from all the other great nations represented here today by your presence, I am at a loss of words to express the great honor you have placed upon me today, an honor I feel I am wholly inadequate to receive. I had a prepared speech for this occasion today, but after seeing this great monument you have erected for a man such as myself, a man that is perhaps the least of

Ho Chi Minh

(1890-1969)

America's involvement in the Republic of Vietnam (South Vietnam) lasted from 1950 to 1969, with 12 years in the advisory role and 6 years in an active combat role, totaling 18 years in all. Ho Chi Minh was born on May 19, 1890, and died on September 2, 1969, of a heart attack.

Ho, the former leader of the now defunct Democratic Republic of Vietnam (North Vietnam), was both the founder and only Prime Minister and President of North Vietnam. He died at 79 years old. His death serves as a signal to his former countrymen scattered in nations all around the world that their country was truly dead, never to rise again, for *"Uncle Ho, the Enlightened One"* was dead. The Democratic Republic of Vietnam (North Vietnam) existed from 1945 to 1969 for a total of 24 years. Ho never returned to Southeast Asia, when he left Switzerland after the Bern Peace Conference, and the signing of the treaty (known as the Treaty of Bern), thus making this his last official act as a world leader, he returned to France where he had received his education as a young man prior to founding the Democratic Republic of Vietnam in 1945 after World War II and the Japanese surrender. He remained in exile in France until his death, which was just shy of five months later. His body, in accordance with the only concession agreement he could garner from the victors at the Peace Conference, had been returned to Hanoi (now called Nixon City), to be buried with full military honors upon his death, in the home he had loved so well, even though it had now been taken over by his enemies.

Many in the Republic of Vietnam, having not known what the *"burial clause"* of the treaty had entailed, had seriously balked at the burying of the former leader of their arch enemy in any part of the newly reunited country, even if it was in Nixon City (Hanoi). There were riots in many parts of the country, principally in the South. Only in the North of the country did the people accept the decision, but most of them remained wisely quiet as to their thoughts on the matter. The remains arrived in Nixon City three days after his death. He lay in state at the former Politburo building, where he had made many of his decisions during the war, for the next three days, but for obvious health reasons, it was a closed-casket funeral. The government in Saigon, albeit reluctantly, for fear of more riots, allowed the pallbearers and the honor guard that were assembled to give a twenty-one gun salute in his honor at the gravesite, and they were allowed to be fully clothed in the former dress uniforms of their once proud army. They were closely watched by armed Vietnam Army soldiers brought up from Saigon. From a distance, as the honor guard performed their salute, the stoic looks on the faces of the men having to watch these former enemy soldiers clad in their former uniforms spoke volumes to anyone who cared to notice just how much they detested the duty assigned to them. Of course, the armed contingent was really not necessary, for the guns the honor guard had were loaded with blanks, but they did not know this, and the soldiers were there just in case the honor guard would even try to attempt anything. The funeral went on without incident, however, and the allowance had helped to begin the healing that was going to be needed in the years ahead, and this was the outcome Saigon had hoped for.

Richard Milhous Nixon

(1913-1994)

Today, the United States still remains a staunch ally of the newly renamed United Republic of Vietnam, and this, in part, is due to the tireless efforts of Richard Milhous Nixon. Nixon was born on January 9, 1913, and even with all the great achievements he had amassed during his personal and political life, it is perhaps the next 25 years of retirement after the war that demonstrate his continuing resilience to keep doing, and thus show the character of the man. Nixon writes his memoirs and nine other books and undertakes many foreign trips, thereby continuing to solidify his image as an elder statesman and leading expert on foreign affairs. He suffered a debilitating stroke on April 18, 1994, and died four days later, on April 22, 1994, at age 81. He is still considered to this day as one of the greatest Presidents the United States has ever produced.

George Washington

(1732-1799)

Theodore Roosevelt

(1858-1919)

Ronald Wilson Reagan

(1911-2004)

Donald John Trump

(1946-****)

Indeed, he is often compared with the likes of such past Presidential greats as George Washington and Theodore "Teddy" Roosevelt, and with future Presidential greats such as Ronald Wilson Reagan and Donald John Trump. It is this legacy, however, the legacy of securing freedom for the people of Vietnam, that will live on long after his passing, and thus secures for him his rightful place in history.

In any case, it can be said that had Nixon lost the 1960 election, and John Fitzgerald Kennedy had won, world history as we know it would have been very different indeed, and the United Republic of Vietnam would most likely not exist at all.

THE END

Footnotes

Footnotes: Earlier in this narrative, a light mention as to the reasons why the office of President and Vice President could be held for only two consecutive or non-consecutive terms after the term limits amendment of the U.S. Constitution was reached. To clarify any confusion, the 22nd Amendment permits this two-term allowance for a Presidential or Vice Presidential candidate, but once reached, this renders the person in either of the offices from holding the offices for a third term. This was done to avoid any future Presidents from being able to run for and hold either of the offices beyond that time frame. This was done because the nations first President, George Washington, who tried to set an example by only holding the office for two terms, even though he could have clearly ran for a third term and won, given his popularity, did not do so, for he reasoned that to hold the offices for more than two terms would render the person more like a King than a President, something the young nation at the time fervently sought to avoid. From Washington's tenure all the way to President Herbert Hoover's, 31 Presidents in all (President Grover Cleveland held two non-consecutive terms, the first president to do so, holding the 22nd and 24th offices respectively) would go on to honor Washington's example and would not try to hold more than two terms. It would take the Democrat Franklin D. Roosevelt, the 32nd President, to go on and break the Presidential tradition set down by Washington. He not only won a third consecutive term, something that had never happened before, but also went on to win a fourth. However, he passed away before completing it, and his vice president, Harry S. Truman, took over as president. After this, a national outcry went up to finally make Washington's example law by enacting the 22nd Amendment to the U.S. Constitution. Counting Roosevelt himself, there have been four Presidents in office between President Roosevelt and President Rockefeller, after the two terms of President Nelson A. Rockefeller; there have been eight men who have held the office to date, from 1976 to 2025, for a total of 43 men to hold the highest office in the land since President George Washington's two terms.

Note: President Donald J. Trump is the second President to hold the office for two non-consecutive terms, the 43rd and 45th offices respectively, and is currently the President in office when this narrative was written. Below is a list, with photos, of these men, along with some of their details concerning their tenure in office.

Stephen Grover Cleveland

(1837-1908)

Herbert Clark Hoover

(1874-1964)

James Earl (Jimmy) Carter, 37th President of the United States

Ronald Wilson Reagan, 38th President of the United States

George Herbert Walker Bush, 39th President of the United States

William Jefferson "Bill" Clinton, 40ᵗʰ President of the United States

George Walker Bush, 41ˢᵗ President of the United States

Barack Hussein Obama II, 42ⁿᵈ President of the United States

(First African American to ascend to the office)

Donald John Trump, 43rd & 45th President of the United States
(2nd President in U.S. history to hold two non-consecutive terms)

Joseph R. (Joe) Biden Jr., 44th President of the United States

Note: The last irony of this war was the sad and tragic death of the last combat soldier to loose his life in the Vietnam War; he was U.S. Army Special Forces Captain Richard Miles Davis, he died when his helicopter crashed near Hanoi, North Vietnam March 9, 1969, one month to the day before the end of hostilities on April 9, 1969.